THE DUKE AND DUCHESS OF DALLAS

A Bulletproof Bond

Tara Ellis

Words on Paper

CHAPTER ONE

Ford was about to turn around and see what Rico was staring at but felt someone hit him in the back of his head with the butt of a gun. The blow sent Ford to the floor, and his gun skidded across the marble floor out of his arm's reach.

Shit! Ford tried to recover quickly and get back to his feet to defend himself against whoever had just snuck him from behind. When he saw who stood behind him, pointing a gun directly in his face, Ford could no longer move. He could barely even breathe.

He wondered if the blow he'd just received to his head had him hallucinating, because now he was seeing ghosts. He was staring into the face of his brother. Ford opened his mouth, but it was a struggle to even speak. He had to know; he had to ask. He forced the words out of his trembling lips.

"Duke? Is it really you, Duke?"

Demarcus frowned down at Ford. How was this little nigga able to get this close to Rico?

"Duke?" Ford blinked back tears as he gaped at his big brother. Emotion had his voice cracking. Was this really happening right now? Was he really staring into the eyes of his brother?

"Naw, nigga. You got me mistaken for somebody else. Just like you were mistaken when you ran up in here pointing that gun in my man's face," Demarcus growled.

Ford wasn't mistaken. He knew he was staring at Duke as surely as he knew he was Black... as surely as he knew his own name.

He gaped at his brother. Yeah, it was definitely Duke. His skin was a little darker from so much time spent on the Dominican beaches. His beard was a lot thicker, his mannerisms a little off, but nevertheless, the man standing above him with his finger on the trigger was definitely his older brother, Duke.

"Duke! What the fuck, man? It's me, Ford!" Ford cried out as he struggled to his feet. He wanted to run up to Duke and hug him like a lost kid finally reunited with his parents, but the way Duke had that gun trained on him gave Ford pause.

Ford couldn't think straight; nothing made any real sense. Duke was alive! He struggled not to break down and cry while also not understanding why Duke was pointing a gun at him, or why Duke glared at him like he'd never seen Ford a day in his life. What the hell was going on?

"You want me to put a bullet in his head right now or what?" Demarcus asked Rico, completely ignoring Ford.

Rico walked over. Of course he was going to have Demarcus kill Ford, but first, he wanted answers. This entire situation wasn't sitting right with him.

Rico placed a hand on Demarcus's shoulder. "Wait one second, Demarcus." He narrowed his eyes at Ford. "I want to know why I was seconds away from being put into a casket. You just saved one of my cargo ships from confiscation, I invite you into my home to reward your ingenious quick thinking, and you put a gun to my fuckin' head." Rico scratched his temple as if the confusion caused him to itch. He glared at the young bull that could have just taken him out the game permanently, and anger pulsed through his blood. Never had anyone gotten this close to him. He was like a god around here, and it had him a little shook to know he'd been so close to meeting the Grim Reaper.

"Ford, is it?" he asked, his accent thicker than ever.

Ford matched Rico's glare with one equally as venomous but didn't answer the man.

"Ford, help me understand your motives here. Who sent you?" Rico demanded.

"Nobody sent me," Ford spat. "You killed my fuckin' brother, so I came to body yo' ass!" As Ford said this, the conviction and wrath that were once so heavy inside of him, were no longer in his voice. Just confusion. Ford shook his head because none of this made any sense.

"I've killed a lot of men," Rico said nonchalantly followed by a slight chuckle. "I need you to be a little more specific here. Just who is your brother?"

Ford returned his eyes to Duke and nudged his head in Duke's direction. "He's my brother."

Wait, what? Brother? Demarcus didn't know what the hell this little nigga was talking about. He lowered his gun and looked over at Rico, who looked just as confused as Demarcus felt.

"Demarcus is your brother?" Rico asked Ford, but he was looking at Demarcus for confirmation of this.

Demarcus stared in silence at Ford, long and hard for what felt like ten minutes.

Rico sized Ford up. There wasn't anything counterfeit about the look on Ford's face or the emotion in his voice. Maybe he was just saying some shit to save his life. If that was the case, he deserved an academy award for his acting abilities because the shock, disbelief, and genuine astonishment on his face was something Rico knew couldn't be faked.

"I don't have a brother," Demarcus finally said, breaking the silence in the room. He spoke as if he knew what he was saying to be a fact. He didn't have a brother. He didn't have *any* family other than Auri and their son. This nigga was lying, and his time was up.

Demarcus lifted his gun and shot Ford twice in the chest. The impact of the bullets sent Ford back to the ground. He felt the hot, searing pain of the bullets, but that was miniscule compared to the pain he felt knowing his brother had just looked him in his eyes and shot him. Demarcus hovered over Ford who was laid out, struggling to breathe. He aimed the gun at Ford's head, ready to silence him and his foolishness forever.

"Duke... Duke... don't. Bro, please don't," Ford pleaded through choked breaths. The tears in his eyes now fell freely down his face.

Before Demarcus could squeeze the trigger a third time, Rico placed his hand on his arm to stop him. "I'll handle him. I need you to get down to the port and take care of that shipment."

Demarcus hesitated before nodding and returning his gun to his waist. He didn't spare Ford another glance as he exited the office. He couldn't wait to get home and tell Auri the crazy ass shit this nigga was up in here saying. Niggas would say anything to save their lives, but this one took the cake! He laughed all the way to his car as he thought about it.

Both of Ford's hands were on his chest. His breathing was erratic, but he knew he wasn't dying. His adrenaline and confusion had him barely able to get enough air into his lungs.

Rico eyed Ford before giving him a hand and helping him to his feet. "You're wearing a vest," he stated.

Ford nodded before ripping open his shirt and pulling the vest off. "I never leave home without it." He walked over to the couch in the corner of the room and sat on it while burying his face into his hands. He knew it wasn't smart to take his eyes off Rico, but at the moment, his thoughts were on what just happened.

"Fuck!" Ford screamed as loud as his vocal cords would

allow. Duke had just shot him! His own brother had just looked at him like he was a stranger and tried to kill him. Ford was shattered. The only other time he'd ever felt this much emotional devastation was the day of Duke's funeral.

"The only reason I didn't let Demarcus put a bullet in your head is because unlike my teniente, I actually believe you," Rico stated from across the room.

Ford looked up from his hands. Rico had noticed the resemblance between Ford and Demarcus. That coupled with the emotion radiating off Ford was enough for Rico to believe everything the young bull claimed. Rico was an expert at reading people. In his line of work, he had to be. He hadn't climbed his way to the top not being able to spot a liar within minutes, and Ford was definitely not a liar. Rico knew that right away. What he didn't know was why Ford would think he'd killed Demarcus.

"You call him Duke?"

Ford nodded.

"We know him as Demarcus. He has a uhh... how can I put this... He's been through a lot," Rico tried to explain.

"What's wrong with him?" Ford asked. "Because the nigga that just walked out of here wasn't my brother. Ain't no way in hell Duke would ever..." Ford couldn't even finish his thought, let alone voice it.

"He has a medical condition that erased all of his memories. He's been like that since I met him."

Ford's confusion distorted his facial features. "Huh? How? I don't understand what the fuck is going on here, man. I thought my brother was dead! I thought you killed him! Come to find out, my bro is alive and well. And what does he do when he sees me? He puts two fuckin' bullets in me!" Ford felt like he was trapped in some other universe, because nothing made any real sense.

Rico took a seat on the edge of his oversized desk. He

grabbed a cigar from the drawer and lit it before speaking. "I don't know everything. I only know what my cousin, Auri, told me. And she's not exactly known for her virtue of truth telling."

Rico always knew Auri was trifling, sneaky, and scheming. He didn't put anything past her. Right now, he had a thousand questions for her ass. He looked at Ford and saw grief and confusion on his face. Under any other circumstance, Ford would have been dead for pulling a gun on him. For the first time in his life, Rico was going to grant a man clemency.

Rico took several puffs of his authentic Cuban cigar before speaking again. "My cousin said his name was Demarcus. She introduced him to me as her fiancé. She said he'd been in a boating accident that caused him some kind of brain damage that erased all of his memories." Rico had known the day Auri came to him that she and the story was flaw. On the strength of her being family, he did her a favor and allowed her boyfriend to work for him. At the time, he had no idea the asset Demarcus would later become to his organization. He definitely didn't think he would become his second-in-command.

"She said they'd been dating for years at the time of his accident," Rico said.

"With all due respect," Ford said, "your cousin is a gotdamn lie. The nigga that just walked out of here is Duke Kingston, and he's my older brother. I thought he was dead. We all thought he was dead. Every fuckin' body thought he was dead. We had a funeral for him and everything." Ford paused to catch his breath. He looked Rico directly in his eyes, searching for treachery. "We thought you killed him."

"Help me understand why you thought I killed Demarcus—or Duke," Rico said.

Ford took a deep breath and ran his hands down his face. "About a year ago, a few members of the clique came down here for Duke's bachelor party. He had a meeting with you, so the timing lined up perfectly. For whatever reason, he and his man, Shai, wouldn't let me and my niggas come along to this meeting which was the dumbest thing he could have ever done because you ended up killing him... or at least that's what we thought happened." Ford paused, trying to remember the story as it had been told to him.

"Shai's pussy thirsty ass got distracted by the hoes you brought along on the boat. I'm not sure how the meeting went sour, but Shai said he heard gunshots, and by the time he made it back up on deck, Duke was nowhere to be found. We figured you shot him and tossed him overboard."

Rico had never heard the names Shai or Duke before today. If this was the story Shai had told Ford, Rico knew just like his cousin, Auri, this Shai character was a liar.

"I have no fuckin' clue what you're talking about. That most certainly never happened. I never had a meeting with Duke or Shai. In fact, the first time I ever met Duke was when my cousin introduced him to me as Demarcus, her fiancé."

Ford's mind was reeling so fast, he felt dizzy. Had Shai lied to him about what happened? Why would Shai make all that up? And who the hell was this Auri? How did she fit into all of this?

Ford wasn't sure if he should even believe anything Rico said. How could he trust this nigga? He spent the better part of last year hating and hunting him. He wasn't about to jump off a cliff and just believe anything he had to say.

As if he could read Ford's mind, Rico put his cigar out and said, "You don't trust me. I get it. You're probably in shock right now. You've been led to believe your brother was dead, by my hands, and you just found out he's not only alive and well but doesn't have a clue who you are. That's a lot to wrap your head around."

Ford was silent as he tried to put reign on his thoughts.

"I can guarantee you I'm going to get to the bottom of all of this, Ford." Rico was already formulating a plan in his head.

Ford struggled with the fact Duke was really alive, but on top of that, he was walking around thinking he was somebody else. He had no memory of who he really was or all the people he'd left behind. Ford had to help his brother. He had to somehow make his brother remember what his mind had erased.

His thoughts immediately went to Duchess. If there was one thing Ford knew, it was how much Duke loved Duchess. They had a connection beyond anything Ford had ever seen. That kind of bond couldn't be broken; that kind of bond was bulletproof.

Duke looked right at Ford and tried to body him, so Ford obviously didn't have the power to help him regain his memories, but he knew the one person in this world who could. Ford had to get in touch with Duchess. Duke needed her now more than ever, or he'd be lost to them all forever.

CHAPTER TWO

Duchess couldn't believe this was really happening to her. Sure, for majority of her life she'd dreamed of singing in front of sold out arenas, but never had she actually believed she would get the chance to do it. Tomorrow, however, she was hopping on a plane to start the first leg of the fifty-city tour with the country's biggest singer, Leela Lennox.

Duchess won a competition to become Leela's background singer. There were so many chart-topping singers who got their start as a background singer, so this was only the beginning of everything Duchess wished and prayed for. The only thing that could make this moment perfect was if Duke was by her side to see her dreams coming to life. Somehow though, Duchess knew Duke was smiling down at her, prouder than ever.

"Bae, you gonna have to leave some of this stuff behind," Brian said, interrupting Duchess's thoughts as he struggled to zip one of her Louis Vuitton suitcases. "This thing has to be way over the weight limit, and it won't zip up."

Duchess looked at Brian and immediately felt guilty for thinking about Duke. She caught herself doing this often when she was with Brian and had to stop herself. Duke was her past, and Brian was her future. Plus, Brian was a good dude. He'd been by her side doing his best to help heal the wound left open by Duke's abrupt departure from her life.

They'd agreed to take things slow in their relationship, but these days, she spent more nights at Brian's place than at her own. He was so different than Duke, but that didn't take away from the feelings she developed for him. It actually made her fall for him even faster. Brian was a straight laced, nine-to-five type dude. He didn't make a fraction of the money Duke had been bringing home, but at least Duchess didn't have to worry about him not making it home in one piece or receiving a collect call from the local jail in the middle of the night.

He didn't invoke the electrical, explosive emotions Duke had birthed inside of Duchess every time he simply smiled at her, but Duchess figured with time, what she had with Brian would grow.

On the other hand, Brian fell fast and hard for Duchess. Never in his life had a woman made him feel the way Duchess did by just looking at him. He was wide open for that woman. His heart was up for her taking. All Duchess had to do was open her hand, and Brian would eagerly place it in her palm.

"Seriously, Duchess. You gonna have to unpack some of this stuff," Brian said, giving up on trying to zip the suitcase.

Billie entered Duchess's bedroom, laughing. "Duch, you packed like you're gonna be gone a whole year."

"Isn't the tour only like three months?" Brian asked.

"Yeah, but I don't know what I'm gonna need. I would rather be overpacked than under packed," Duchess said.

"Well, I can guarantee you're not gonna need these," Billie said as she pulled a pair of glittery Louboutins from one of Duchess's suitcases. "Or these." She pulled three more pair of extremely high-heeled shoes from the bag and was then able to successfully zip it.

Duchess shrugged. "You never know."

Brian laughed and pulled Duchess into his arms. He kissed her forehead before smiling down at her. Damn, he loved this woman. How was it possible for him to feel such strong emotions in such a short amount of time?

"I'm proud of you, Duchess. You out here chasing your dreams and making them a reality," he told her.

Duchess melted into Brian's embrace. Since winning the competition, she'd lost count of the times Brian said he was proud of her, but she didn't get tired of hearing it. She still hadn't reconciled with her mother, and she no longer talked to Jerrika, so all she had now was Brian and Billie. After a horrible year of heartache and loss, it felt good to have their support and hear someone was proud of her.

After loving Duke with her entire being and then suffering the loss of such a love, Duchess didn't think it would be possible to love another man. Brian was proof there were second chances in life.

"Go sing ya heart out, baby," Brian said. "But I can't lie; I'm gonna miss the shit outta you while you're gone."

"I'm gonna miss you too, baby," she cooed before kissing him. The kiss was supposed to be a short peck but ended up a full tongue wrestle.

"Eeew! If y'all gon' be on that shit, I'ma just gone and leave now," Billie said.

Duchess stuck her tongue out. "It's too early in the day for the hate, Billie."

"Never been a hater a day in my life," Billie said. "What you need to be doing is getting these suitcases together. Your flight leaves at six in the morning, and you know you're not a morning person at all. So your shit needs to be packed and ready today if you wanna catch your flight in time."

Duchess reluctantly pulled away from Brian's hold. Billie was right. She needed to get her bags packed and ready for her early morning flight. She knelt and started going through her bags.

Billie began helping Duchess and couldn't help but smile.

11

She was so proud of her girl, tears almost came to her eyes. From the outside looking in, it looked like Duchess had it all. No one would ever be able to guess her story by just looking at her, but Billie had a front row seat to Duchess's swift and hard fall. So she was getting emotional because she was about to also witness Duchess slowly climb her way back to grace.

"I'm so happy for you, girl," she said. "If anybody deserves this, it's you, Duch."

"Thanks, Billie," Duchess said. "Now stop before you have me in here crying."

"Well, I'll leave y'all to packing. I'm gonna run to the store," Brian said. "Y'all need anything?"

"No. We're good, babe," Duchess said. She smiled to herself as she watched Brian leave. Yeah, she was definitely going to miss him while on tour.

Fifteen minutes later, Duchess still debated what she absolutely couldn't leave behind, when her cell phone started ringing. She froze as soon as she saw the name on the display.

Ford.

It'd been a long time since she'd last spoken to Ford, so to see him calling was a complete shock. What in the world did Ford have to say to her now after all this time? She debated if she should even answer the call.

Billie noticed the look on Duchess's face. "Who is that?"

"Ford."

Billie sat up straighter. "Ford? What does he want?"

"I don't know."

"Well, answer it and see."

Duchess's finger hovered over the call accept button for so long, the phone stopped ringing.

"I haven't talked to Ford in... forever. I have no idea why he's calling me now."

"You gonna call him back?" Billie asked, a little curious as to what Ford wanted. It'd been over a year since they'd last seen or heard from him.

"Naw." Duchess decided almost immediately. It wasn't anything against Ford. She just preferred to leave that chapter of her life in the past. Talking to him now would only sour her mood and leave her thinking about Duke for the rest of the day.

"Y'all need some help in there?" Brian called from the living room couch. He was watching a football game.

"No!" Duchess and Billie said in unison.

The last thing Duchess wanted was for Brian to know Ford had just called her. Brian had a few insecurities surrounding her relationship with Duke. He knew how much she'd loved Duke, and to make matters worse, it wasn't like their relationship ended on bad terms. Duke didn't leave Duchess for another woman; he hadn't cheated and broken her heart. He'd been killed. So to Brian, Duchess would forever love Duke.

"Did he leave a voicemail?" Billie asked.

Duchess was just about to check her voicemail when the phone started ringing again.

"Is that him again?" Billie asked.

Duchess nodded. For Ford to call her back-to-back, it had to be important. She accepted the call with full apprehension.

"Hello?"

"Duchess?" Ford sounded like he was out of breath.

"Yeah, it's me."

Ford let out a long breath of relief. "Good. I was worried like hell you wouldn't have the same number."

"No, I never changed it." Duchess felt awkward all of a sudden. "It's been a minute, Ford. What's up? Is everything OK?"

"Uh, not really, Duchess." Ford didn't know where to start. His mind was still reeling. "I'm in the Dominican Republic. I've been living here for a while now. Remember I told you I was coming down here after that nigga Rico?"

"Yeah, I remember," Duchess said, holding her breath.

"Well, I found him."

Duchess released the breath she held. She knew if Ford found Rico and was alive to tell her about it, then Rico was dead. She let the realization hit her. She waited to feel gratification at knowing the man who stole Duke from her was also dead now. It bubbled in the center of her stomach until a smile crept on her face.

"But he wasn't the only one I found. Duchess, I also found Duke."

The phone slipped from Duchess's hand. Both of her hands flew to her mouth, keeping her from screaming. She scrambled to pick her phone back up while ignoring Billie, who was asking a thousand questions.

With hands that wouldn't stop trembling, Duchess brought her phone back to her ear. "Wait, wait, Ford! Slow down."

Tears fell down her cheeks. She'd lost count of how many times she'd prayed for Duke's body to be found. She wanted her man to have a proper burial. She felt he at least deserved that since his life had been prematurely cut short. Now, Ford was telling her the prayer had finally been answered. Maybe with this piece of closure, she'd be able to close the chapter on Duke and Duchess forever.

Emotion had Ford's voice unsteady. "I found him, Duchess. I found him."

"Thank God," Duchess said, releasing a long breath of relief. "How soon can you get his body back to the States so we can bury him?"

"Bury him?" It took Ford a few seconds to realize Duchess thought he'd found Duke's *body*. "No, no, no, Duchess. I found Duke. I found him *alive!*"

Duchess's mind went blank with confusion, not understanding what Ford was trying to tell her. But her heart understood every word, and it now ached to be reunited with its owner.

"Wha-what?" Her mouth was suddenly so dry that it was hard to speak. "What, Ford? How? I don't understand."

I don't know," Ford said. "Shit's crazy as hell to explain. I mean, I'm still trying to wrap my head around the shit."

The emotion in Ford's voice was enough to convince Duchess he wasn't losing his mind. She looked up at Billie, who was trying to rip the phone from her hands for an explanation.

"What the fuck is going on, Duchess?" Billie asked. The look on Duchess's face had Billie sitting on pins and needles.

"Duke... Ford says Duke is alive," Duchess told her.

Billie suddenly felt unsteady on her feet. She slid down the wall until she, too, was seated on the floor.

"He is, Duchess. I've seen and talked to him. He's been down here the whole time. He was never dead." For the first time since being reunited with his brother, Ford cried.

"How? How could Duke be alive and living in the Dominican Republic? What about all of us thinking he was dead? What about *me*? How could he do this to *me*?" Duchess was no longer sitting on the floor. She was now up on her feet, pacing the room at a rapid speed that matched the erratic beating of her heart.

"This is where shit gets crazy, Duch. I don't know what

happened to Duke on that boat with Shai and Rico, but whatever happened really fucked him up. He has some kinda brain damage and doesn't remember shit. He thinks his name is Demarcus or some shit. He doesn't even know who the fuck I am."

"Wait, slow down, Ford." Duchess had to sit back down. Her brain was in overdrive, trying to process everything. She knew she was in shock and wasn't sure how she hadn't passed out from it yet.

"He lost his memory, Duchess. He thinks he's somebody else. He doesn't remember shit about his life in Dallas. He needs *you*. He needs to see you. He needs his Duchess."

"Oh my God!" Duchess said as tears continued to fall down her face. She didn't need time to think about it. There wasn't even a question about it. "I'll be there tomorrow."

Ford knew he could count on Duchess. "Bet," he said. "Text me your flight details, and I'll be there to pick you up when you land."

"OK," Duchess said, and she was already across the room opening her laptop to buy a flight ticket. Her hands trembled, her heart raced, and sweat beads ruined her perfectly laid edges.

"Can you believe this shit, Duchess? We got him back. We got Duke back," Ford said.

Duchess was smiling when she ended the call. Just like that, her life had completely changed in the most incredible way. She couldn't have prayed for something so amazing. She wouldn't have ever let her mind even wish for something so miraculous.

Her thoughts were interrupted by Billie throwing a thousand questions at her. When she looked up from her laptop, it was the first time she'd noticed Brian now stood in the room. His face full of questions, and was that also hurt?

"What the fuck is going on, Duchess?" Billie asked.

"I don't know," she said, "but Duke is alive. Ford found him. He talked to him and everything."

"Huh? Wait, what?" Billie was confused as hell.

"He's alive?" Brian asked. He tried to keep his face neutral, but it was a battle he was losing miserably.

"Ford found him. Oh my God, my baby is alive!" Duchess said. She couldn't contain the overwhelming joy pumping through the blood in her veins. She couldn't contain it if she tried, and right now, she wasn't even trying.

Billie could tell Duchess had no idea what she'd just said or how her words were like knives to Brian's heart. At the same time, she also couldn't blame her girl. All this time, she'd thought the love of her life was dead and gone. But he wasn't...? None of this made any real sense to Billie.

"OK," Billie said slowly as if talking slowly would make any of this more sensible. "If Duke is alive, where has he been all this time? Why did he have us thinking he was dead all this time? I mean, we had a funeral and everything for him."

Duchess shook her head and wiped at the tears on her cheeks. "I don't know all the details right now, Billie, but Ford said he lost his memory. He doesn't even know who he is. He thinks he's someone else. I don't know how any of this is possible. All I do know is I gotta get down there." She hit purchase on the extremely expensive last-minute flight to the Dominican Republic. Coincidentally, her flight to the Dominican Republic was leaving at the same time as her flight to New York to begin the tour with Leela Lennox.

"What! You're going down there?" Billie asked. "You're supposed to be leaving tomorrow to go on tour with Leela Lennox!" Billie felt like she had to remind Duchess of this because she'd clearly forgotten.

Duchess froze. In the excitement of Ford's news, she had

forgotten about the tour with Leela Lennox. She was so close to seeing her biggest dream to fruition, but that dream was once again going to be put on the backburner. Truthfully, she didn't really care.

"I can't. How can I go on this tour knowing Duke is alive out there? I have to get to him," she said as if it shouldn't have even needed an explanation.

Brian wanted to say something, but he felt so frozen by shock that even if he opened his mouth, he knew nothing would come out. Duchess was about to walk out of his life and run into the arms of the man he couldn't even compete with in death, so he knew for sure that in life, Duke had won.

Billie stared open mouthed at Duchess, but what could she say? She knew better than anyone just how much Duchess loved Duke. It didn't matter what was at stake right now. Duchess was going to throw it all away without hesitation for Duke. Billie only hoped Duchess knew what she was doing.

CHAPTER THREE

Demarcus walked into the home he shared with his wife and young son. They both greeted him at the door with identical smiles, full of joy at his arrival. It was something Demarcus could never get enough of. The way his wife's eyes lit up every time he came home was like she expected each time to be the last. His baby boy, Levi, was always a ball of energy when Demarcus came home and scooped him into his arms. Demarcus loved his life; it couldn't get any better than this.

"Welcome home, papi," Auri greeted before kissing him. "You're just in time. Maybe now I can finish dinner without having to chase this lil' bad ass around the house."

"Hey," Demarcus said with a smile, "my lil' nigga ain't bad. You hear the way ya mama talkin' about you, Levi?"

Levi answered his father with sounds of intelligible garbles and a goofy grin on his pudgy face. Demarcus's heart melted every time he laid eyes on his son who seemed to be growing faster by the day. It seemed like just last week, he was keeping them up all night, crying. Now, he was pulling himself up and even trying to walk.

Demarcus followed Auri into the kitchen where she was chopping onions and mincing garlic on a wood cutting board.

"How was your day?" she asked him.

"Crazy as hell," Demarcus said while putting Levi onto the colorful blanket on the floor surrounded by toys.

"Really?" Auri questioned, but she half-listened. Her eyes were glued to the reality show playing on the living room TV. Her eyes only left the TV to ensure she wouldn't cut herself while dicing the onions.

"Rico almost got killed today. I don't even know how the lil' nigga was able to get that close to Rico."

This got Auri's attention. Her cousin was invincible to her, so to hear he was almost killed had her shocked. She looked at Demarcus, waiting for him to finish the story.

Demarcus shook his head as he walked to their oversized stainless-steel refrigerator and grabbed a bottle of water. "I walked in just in time to put the nigga on his ass. Auri, I'm telling you, if I had been even a minute late, Rico woulda been dead." Demarcus could hardly believe it. It was the closest call he'd ever experienced.

"Oh my God! You're lying!" Auri said as her hand went to her mouth.

"No shit. It was crazy as hell. But get this. Guess why this fool said he was trying to get at Rico?"

Auri shrugged. Her cousin's list of enemies was longer than her Nordstrom's receipt after a shopping spree.

"Because Rico killed his brother. And the nigga was up in there claiming I was his brother." Demarcus laughed as if he'd just heard a joke from his favorite standup comedian. He was laughing so hard, he didn't notice how pale Auri's face had gone or how her hand now trembled so bad she had to set the knife on the counter.

"What?" she asked, hoping she'd somehow heard Demarcus wrong.

Demarcus stopped laughing long enough to talk. "Nigga claimed I was his brother." He started laughing again. "I guess he thought that was gonna somehow save his life."

"Wh-why would he say you're his brother?" Auri stuttered.

Demarcus shrugged. "Niggas will say anything when their life is flashing before their eyes."

Auri's mouth was so dry, it was a real effort for her to speak. "What else did he say?"

"I bodied him before he could say any more bullshit."

A powerful surge of relief hit Auri, almost causing her knees to buckle. Every day she lived with the fear Demarcus would regain his memory. She had to live daily with the fear her perfect fairytale life would be snatched away by those memories, so she worked extremely hard to keep them repressed. She'd studied up on Demarcus's condition and learned that as long as she continued to feed him fake memories, the harder it would be for any of his real memories to surface. Never had she taken in account someone from Demarcus's past popping into their lives. Their presence could be detrimental to the life she'd built with Demarcus.

She remembered the friends he was in the club celebrating with the night she met him, but she didn't worry about them coming to look for him. It'd been a year and a half and no one ever came, so she figured no one ever would. She'd lied to Demarcus for so long, she'd even started to believe he really didn't have any family.

Fear paralyzed her. If Demarcus's brother had found him, that meant someone was in fact out there searching for him, and there very well were others.

"What's wrong?" Demarcus asked after finally noticing the way Auri looked. She looked as if she were on the verge of passing out. "You feeling alright?"

"Uh, yeah, I'm good," she said quickly while forcing a smile. The smile was shaky at best. She was suddenly a nervous wreck. Her perfect little life was in jeopardy. She had to think fast and eliminate the threat before any more damage could be done.

"Shit crazy, huh," Demarcus said, still shaking his head. If it wasn't for Auri, he probably would have given the little nigga the benefit of the doubt, but Auri had told him he didn't have any family. For a while, that bothered him. He felt alone in this world, with no memories of his life other than what Auri could tell him.

Thank God for Auri.

He looked at his wife and smiled. He owed her so much. When he didn't have a clue what his name was, she was there for him. When he stared into a mirror and couldn't even recognize his own fucking face, she was there. He was at his absolute lowest, but Auri was there. She helped him back to life every step of the way. He would forever love her for that.

That night, Auri was unusually quiet during dinner. Demarcus could tell she had a lot on her mind, so he volunteered to bathe Levi and put him to bed while she sorted out whatever bothered her.

While Demarcus and Levi were in the bathroom, Auri stepped outside on their patio to call Rico. Usually, the sound of the ocean waves calmed her, but tonight, her nerves were fried. Not even the two glasses of wine she'd had with dinner eased her stress. She was a mess.

"Yeah." Rico answered the call sounding irritated as if he'd been interrupted doing something important.

"Hey, Rico, it's Auri."

"I know!" he snapped. "What do you want?"

Auri had to bite back the sharp response on the edge of her

tongue. She reminded herself that her cousin was almost killed today, so it was no wonder he was in a shitty mood.

"I was calling to see what happened today. Demarcus told me some guy was claiming to be his brother," she feigned concern for Rico, "and he tried to kill you?"

Rico chuckled. He'd been expecting Auri's call. He was only surprised it took her this long. She was trying to get information without showing her hand. Sneaky little bitch.

"Cut the shit, Auri."

Auri was silent. She didn't know how to respond to Rico, so she didn't say anything.

"You have completely fucked up this time."

"I—I don't know what you're talking about," she stuttered.

"Do you have any idea who Demarcus really is?" Rico asked, cutting right to what he wanted to know. "Please tell me you didn't know—that you aren't that fuckin' stupid to play with a man like Duke Kingston."

Duke Kingston? This was the first time Auri had heard Demarcus's real name. She could have gone the rest of her life without hearing it. She didn't want to think about the man he was before she met him.

"Help me understand what the hell is going on, Auri. And think long and hard before you lie to me again, cousin. I know Demarcus wasn't your fiancé before he lost his memory. I know everything you've told me about him was a bold-faced lie. So now I want the truth," Rico said, "all of it."

There was no point in lying now. Rico obviously knew her hand, so she laid her cards on the table. "OK." She sighed. "You're right. I lied. Demarcus wasn't my fiancé before he lost his memory. When I met him, he had no idea who he was."

"So let me get this straight." Rico could hardly believe Auri.

"You find a man with amnesia and feed him a false identity? What, you thought you were gonna just ride off into the sunset with him? Is that what you were thinking, Auri? Please tell me you are not that stupid, little cousin."

Rico didn't give Auri a chance to get a word in edgewise. "You tricked him into believing he was someone he wasn't! How could you not think this would blow up in your face?"

How could Auri explain it to Rico? No matter what she said, he would never understand her motives. To this day, she barely understood why she even did what she did. When she laid eyes on Demarcus in the hospital with no memory of who he really was, all she could remember was that night in the club. How he'd been fiercely loyal to his fiancée, who was thousands of miles away. Auri yearned to know what that kind of love and loyalty felt like. It was something she'd only seen in movies, so when the opportunity to experience it came firsthand, she took it.

Rico would never understand what it felt like to want something so bad for so long and never be able to take hold of it. He was a man that always got any and everything he wanted, so Auri knew trying to make him understand would be pointless.

"You are fuckin' insane!" Rico howled. "He has a real family, Auri—a real life back in the States that you've kept him away from for whatever sick reason."

"A real family? If they cared about him so much, why did they leave him here for dead!" Auri shouted. "It's been a year and a half and someone finally shows up looking for him. You call that family, Rico? Because I definitely do not! Me and Levi are Demarcus's family."

Rico snorted. "Demarcus isn't just some poor guy you happened to come across that has amnesia. Of all the men to play with, you went and fucked with Duke Kingston."

The name Duke Kingston meant nothing to Auri. Before today, she'd never heard the name before. "And? So what?"

"He's a made man in the States, Auri. You fucked up when you chose to play this game with him."

Auri's blood ran cold. She knew the night she first laid eyes on Demarcus in the club, he was someone of importance. She could tell by the way he carried himself and by the way the men with him regarded him with high esteem. Still, that wasn't enough to give her pause that day in the hospital. If anything, it made her want him more.

"If he's such an important man, why didn't you recognize him when I first brought him to you?" Auri asked.

"I don't work with the Americans, Auri. You know this. So after talking to Duke's brother today, I had my people look into his story. So imagine my surprise *and* horror when I found out the guy I've known as my cousin's husband is a drug kingpin in Dallas, Texas!" It was hard for Rico to contain the anger he had for his cousin. She'd put him in a fucked-up predicament.

"He has a real organization, Auri. And once they get wind of what you've done, it's going to bring trouble right to my doorstep."

"How? Demarcus told me he killed the guy who claimed to be his brother. That should be the end of it. Thousands of people come to the DR every year and don't return home. Why should this be any different?"

Rico chuckled before he spoke very condescendingly to Auri. "Demarcus thinks he killed the guy, but he's very much so alive and well."

Auri sucked in air. That was a plot twist she wasn't expecting.

"And now he knows his brother is alive and living in the Dominican Republic. How long do you think it will be before he brings the rest of his team down here?"

Tears welled in Auri's eyes. She could see the fairytale life she'd built for herself crumbling down.

"You can't let that happen, Rico! You have to stop him!"

Rico laughed heartily. "You have got to be using my product if you think I would get any further involved in this nonsense you have created."

"Rico, please! This is my life!"

"You got yourself into this mess, so you better find your way out of it. Good luck!"

He ended the call while Auri was still begging for his help.

CHAPTER FOUR

Ford was a sight for sore eyes, and Duchess's eyes were definitely sore from all the crying she'd been doing since hearing Duke was alive. She dropped her luggage and ran up to Ford. She wrapped her arms around him, hugging him as tight as she could. If it hadn't been for him, she'd still be thinking Duke was gone forever.

It felt like Duchess was never going to let him go. Ford laughed. "It's good seeing you too, sis."

Duchess was just about to wipe the tears from her face when she noticed Tommy and Gunz standing behind Ford. It'd been a long time, but the twin boys in front of her no longer looked like little kids. Even Ford looked like a grown ass man. So much had changed. Nostalgia hit as she remembered them always tagging behind Duke every chance they got.

"Oh my God! Tommy! Gunz! It feels like forever since I seen y'all. Come here." She hugged both of them, grateful to be reunited with such a huge piece of her past.

Tommy picked up Duchess's suitcase, and they headed toward the exit of the airport.

"This shit crazy as hell, huh, Duch?" Tommy asked.

Duchess swiped at her tears. "Crazy isn't even the word. I know Ford has told me the story like five times, and my brain still hasn't really processed any of it."

When they made it through the airport and got inside Ford's car, Duchess could barely sit still. Anxious energy bounced off her at the thought of seeing Duke again. It was like her body knew she was in the proximity of her love.

"You need to prepare yourself for what you're about to see, Duchess," Ford said as he pulled off the parking lot. "The Duke I seen yesterday ain't our Duke."

Ford had already told Duchess this for what felt like a thousand times. She already knew Duke lost his memory and probably wouldn't recognize her. None of that mattered to her right now. She just needed to see him.

"He thinks he's somebody else," Gunz said from the back seat. "Nigga tried to kill Ford and everything."

"What?" Duchess's neck snapped in Ford's direction. That, he hadn't told her.

Ford frowned at Gunz in the rearview, and Gunz only shrugged.

"Yeah," he said. "He shot me. Twice. That's why I'm tellin' you the nigga you're about to see now isn't Duke. His head is real fucked-up."

Duchess sucked in air. She hadn't been expecting that. If Duke would pull a gun on Ford and even go as far as to pull the trigger, maybe he was more far gone than she was prepared for.

"I don't trust that nigga Rico either," Gunz said. "I say we get Duke and get the fuck out this country as soon as possible. Ford put a gun to Rico's head, and I don't care what he says. A man like Rico ain't quick to forgive some shit like that."

Duchess looked at Ford. "Are we in danger?"

Ford waved his hand to dismiss what Gunz had just said. "Don't listen to this nigga's paranoia. We good. Ain't shit gonna happen to none of us."

Duchess wanted to find comfort in Ford's words, but she had to agree with Gunz. "Well, just in case, let's get Duke and get back home."

"There's a lot of shit you don't know yet, Duch," Ford said. "Shit ain't gonna be that simple."

"How do you know we can trust Rico? This is the same man we thought had killed Duke."

"My point exactly," Gunz said.

Tommy elbowed him to silence him.

"He didn't kill Duke though," Ford pointed out. "Duke is alive and working for Rico. I mean, he's Rico's lieutenant and everything. I'm not saying I trust the nigga, but I don't think he had anything to do with what happened to Duke."

"What exactly happened to Duke?" Duchess asked.

"Man, Duch, I don't really know. All I know is my brother looked me right in my eye and didn't know who the fuck I was."

Chills ran down Duchess's back. She wasn't sure what she expected to happen when she was finally able to lay eyes on Duke, but she hoped with everything inside of her, he would somehow know who she was. She couldn't imagine any other outcome of their reunion.

"The nigga has some kind of amnesia like in the movies," Tommy offered. "That shit be temporary though, right?"

"Nigga, do we look like doctors? How the hell we supposed to know?" Gunz cracked.

Duchess tried to participate in the conversation, but her mind was all over the place. Her body was reacting to the knowledge that in just a mere hour or so, she was going to be reunited with the love of her life. Her pulse quickened, and her heartbeat tripled in speed. Ford and the twins tried to mentally prepare her for Duke's amnesia, but she barely paid them any attention. The kind of love she and Duke shared could cure the deadliest disease, so she fully expected Duke's memory to return as soon as he laid eyes on her.

When the car pulled into the driveway of an extravagant mansion, Duchess knew it had to be Rico's home. She was apprehensive as she got out of the car and followed Ford and the twins inside.

She tried not to let what Gunz said earlier get to her. She didn't trust Rico, but she did trust Ford's judgement, and she didn't think he would lead them into a trap.

Rico greeted them in the large, stark-white foyer. He looked exactly how Duchess imagined. He was of average height, slim, and immaculately dressed in a tailored suit. His jet-black hair was gelled to perfection with a neatly trimmed beard and dark mysterious eyes under a set of thick eyebrows.

"You must be Duchess," Rico said as he took her hand and kissed it.

Even though Duchess now knew Rico hadn't murdered the love of her life, she still recoiled at his touch. The last year of hating this man with everything inside of her couldn't be so easily erased.

Rico didn't seem to notice Duchess's reaction to him because he just stood there smiling at her, wondering how the hell Demarcus could have ever forgotten a woman this beautiful.

"Ford has told me so much about you. It's a pleasure to be able to put a beautiful face to the stories."

Duchess wanted to offer a fake smile, but she couldn't even do that. She hated this man, and her face just wouldn't cooperate.

"Ford tells me you once meant a lot to Demarcus—or Duke, as you know him," Rico said. "We're hoping you will be able to help him with his memory loss," Rico said.

"Where is he?' Duchess asked, growing impatient. She was ready to see her man. She needed to see him with her own eyes to believe he was really still alive. The last thing she wanted to do was chop it up with this man, the man she'd thought was responsible for Duke's death.

"I'm sure you're ready to reunite with him, but I have to warn you. He has no memory of being Duke at all, so please try and prepare yourself." Rico led them into his den. "Would you all like something to drink?"

"Sure," she said, needing something strong to take the edge off. She was on the verge of a panic attack. She looked around the flawlessly decorated den and admired Rico's taste. This man was obviously a boss. Everything about his home bragged of his status.

"I'm good," Gunz growled. He didn't give a damn what Ford said, he didn't trust this nigga. He fingered the gun hid in his waistband, fully expecting he'd have to use it before leaving this house today.

"Me too," Ford said. He didn't need alcohol clouding his head right now.

Tommy opted for the same thing Duchess was drinking, which was the best cognac Rico had in his bar. He dropped a few cubes of ice into the drinks and handed them the glasses.

Duchess took the drink with shaky hands and sipped it slowly, while her mind went a mile a minute.

"Duke will be here shortly," Rico said as he eyed Duchess. He admired her beauty without coming off creepy. He'd had his share of beautiful women, and Duchess definitely was a pleasure to look at. If Demarcus couldn't remember being Duke after one look at this woman, Rico considered shooting his shot with the dark-skinned beauty.

Duchess nervously sipped the drink while her eyes scanned the room, continuously returning to the door in anticipation of Duke walking through it. She had to keep reminding herself to breathe because she kept holding her breath in expectation. She had too much nervous energy bouncing around inside of her to remain seated. She stood and paced the room.

Rico was about to try to make small talk, when the door finally opened, and Demarcus entered.

It was as if everything began moving in slow motion. Duchess felt all the air leave her lungs. She felt lightheaded, and her knees went wobbly and weak. If it hadn't been for Ford, who stood close enough to catch her as she was falling, she would have collapsed right onto the hardwood floors beneath her.

Demarcus's eyes went from the twins, who were posted up next to Ford. He immediately recognized Ford from yesterday, so his head snapped in Rico's direction. "Rico, what the fuck?" He didn't give the fainting woman a second glance or thought.

"Please, have a seat, Demarcus. I need to speak with you," Rico quickly said before Demarcus's temper had the chance to make an appearance.

Demarcus hesitated. He thought Rico had taken care of this lying ass nigga, so why was he still breathing and standing in Rico's den as if Demarcus hadn't put two in his chest.

"The fuck going on here?" Demarcus wanted to know. He looked back at the twins, who gawked at him as if he'd come back from the dead or something. Then, he focused his attention on Ford who struggled to revive the woman who had passed out. Finally, he looked at Rico. "Tell me something, man."

"Just sit down, and I'll explain everything to you," Rico said.

"I think it's better if I stand right here."

"Fine," Rico said, shrugging. He looked at Ford and handed him a small glass of water. "Here, splash this in her face."

Duchess's eyes fluttered open as soon as the cold water hit her. It took her a few seconds to remember where she was. As soon as she did, she jolted upright, her eyes dancing across the room until they landed on Duke.

Her Duke.

She opened her mouth to speak, but nothing came out.

Concern distorted Ford's facial features. He expected Duchess to freak out when she saw Duke, but he didn't expect her to faint. He didn't want her to stand up because he feared she'd do it again. "You alright, Duchess?"

She nodded. She was more than alright. She was complete.

"Demarcus, I have reason to believe your name isn't really Demarcus Jones but Duke Kingston. And this is Ford. He really is your brother. This is Duchess, your fiancée," Rico said.

Demarcus didn't even look at Ford or Duchess because he was glaring at Rico. "Man, Rico, what the fuck you talkin' about? You let this lil' nigga game you like that?" Demarcus shook his head. He couldn't believe Rico. He was supposed to be the king of the Dominican, and he'd been suckered too easily.

Rico shook his head. "You know me better than that."

"It's true," Ford said as he stood and walked closer to Demarcus. He knew he was taking a gamble with his life by doing so, but he had to bring his brother back. He reached into his wallet and pulled out two photos. He lifted his hand to give them to Demarcus, but Demarcus just stared at Ford's hands as if he were trying to hand him a pile of dog shit.

Rico cleared his throat. "When you left yesterday, I took the liberty of looking into Ford's story. It checks out, Demarcus. Everything he said was true."

Demarcus's glare didn't waver.

"Just look at the pictures, man," Ford said, almost pleading.

Demarcus snatched the pictures from Ford, glanced down at them, and then back up to Ford. Something on the photo made him look back at it. He stared into the face of his own. He was smiling in the photo with his arm around the same dude claiming to be his brother. The realization this might not be bullshit after all had Demarcus feeling unsteady on his feet.

Gunz had his eyes on Rico. As bad as he wanted to watch Duke's reactions, he had to keep his eyes on Rico. He didn't trust him and wouldn't let him catch them slipping. He was fully prepared to pop off if need be. In fact, he itched to do so.

Tommy stood in disbelief. He'd quickly finished the cognac and now he wished he had a second one. Duke was alive, but he really had no idea who any of them were! Hearing the story from Ford was one thing, but seeing it with his own eyes had him tripped out.

Duchess couldn't remain seated anymore. She jumped from the couch and rushed toward Duke. She stumbled under the weight of the unbelievable. Her man was alive. Her man was right here in front of her. She reached for him; she had to touch him. Demarcus snatched out of her reach. He looked up at her, and even though he was laying eyes on her for the first time, he could tell by her reaction to his presence that this woman loved him. Deeply.

He stumbled backward until his back was against the wall, literally and figuratively. He felt like a trapped animal. Everyone in the room stared at him, expecting him to say something, but he couldn't even formulate a complete thought, let alone a sentence.

He'd just learned everything he believed to be true was a lie.

"I know this is a lot for you, Duke," Duchess said, finally being able to speak. Her voice was shaky and barely above a whisper. Tears raced down her face. She could tell he didn't want to be touched by her, so it took everything inside of her not to rush him, grab him, shake him, hold him, kiss him.

Demarcus looked back at the photos Ford had given him.

In the second picture, he was photo'd with Ford and the same twins in the room right now. He was laughing. He appeared to be happy. In his past, he'd known all these people. He looked to Rico for answers, pleading to understand what was going on.

Rico sighed. "My fuckin' cousin!" He spat the words as if they tasted nasty on his tongue. "She lied to you. She lied to me. All of us."

Demarcus felt like if he didn't sit down soon, he would pass out just like Duchess had done earlier. He walked over to the couch but felt no relief once he'd sat down.

Duchess was by his side in seconds. She grabbed his hands, unable to be so close to him a second longer and not touch him. She wanted to scream, cry, fall to her knees, and thank God for answering a prayer she hadn't even had enough faith to pray.

Demarcus stared blankly at Duchess. Even with the red, puffy eyes and black mascara running down her face, she was one of the most beautiful women he'd ever lain eyes on.

"Somebody wanna tell me what the fuck is going on?" he asked.

"Like Rico said, your name ain't no Demarcus or whatever the fuck they got you believing down here. You're Duke Kingston. My older brother, the fucking Duke of Dallas! We don't know what happened to you or why you down here thinkin' you somebody else. All we know is we all thought you were dead," Ford explained.

"Yeah, you thought Rico killed me," Demarcus said, remembering what Ford had said yesterday. Now he heard it in a different light because he now knew there was actually truth to what he'd said. Knowing that made Demarcus sick to his stomach for a host of reasons, but the main one being he'd tried to kill Ford yesterday. His brother. What if he'd succeeded? He would have unknowingly murdered his own flesh and blood. His stomach felt hollow.

"Auri lied to you, Demarcus..." Rico said, searching for the right way to break it to him but coming up short with ideas. So, he just gave it to him straight without a chaser. "She lied about everything. I don't know how she did it, but she convinced you that you were someone else."

"Why would Auri do that?" Demarcus asked, not wanting to accept what was obviously true. "Why would Auri do that to me?"

Rico shrugged. "That's the million-dollar question."

"Who is Auri?" Duchess asked.

Ford shifted uncomfortably. This was the part he'd opted to leave out of the story. He couldn't bring himself to tell Duchess that Duke had married some other woman. Even if he did it while not knowing who he was, that shit was going to kill Duchess.

"It don't matter," Ford said quickly before Rico or Demarcus could tell her.

"So, my name is Duke?" Demarcus said more to himself than to anyone in the room. He looked at Ford long and hard. Why hadn't he noticed the resemblance they shared before now? "And you're my brother?"

Ford nodded.

"And I'm your fiancée," Duchess blurted out. She could no longer stop herself. She wrapped her arms around Duke's neck and held onto him tight, like if she didn't, he would disappear into thin air. She held onto him in the way she wished she could all those lonely nights after his funeral. She held onto him like she'd done his pillows those same lonely, miserable nights, because they still smelled of him. She broke down in Duke's arms, crying for all the time they'd lost. Her sobs were gut wrenching because they came from a place of loss and redemption.

Demarcus was caught completely off guard, but he held

onto the woman as she sobbed so hard, her entire body shook. He looked at Rico and mouthed the words, "What the fuck?"

He felt awkward with this woman who wasn't Auri, in his arms. Even though he was mad as hell at her right now, all he knew was Auri's body, so the woman in his arms felt like a stranger.

Duchess could have stayed in Duke's arms forever. It'd been so long, but she never forgot the way it felt to be wrapped inside his arms. The smell of his skin and how her body felt against the hardness of his muscular chest—some things were engraved into her memory. She thought it would forever only be a memory, but here she was, once again in the arms of the man her soul belonged to.

When she finally pulled away and released Duke, she gawked at him like she still didn't believe he was real. Everything Duchess had ever felt for Duke came rushing back with the force of a speeding train. The sensation of homecoming and a bond that refused to break had her refusing to look away from him.

She watched Duke's facial expression go from anger and confusion to disbelief.

"You don't remember me at all?" she asked him, even though she could tell by the way he stared blankly back at her, he didn't.

On the plane ride here, Duchess read fifty different articles about amnesia, but none of that was enough to prepare her for this. She was barely able to recover from Duke being alive, but now she had to cope with him having no idea who she was.

Still, she would take his memory loss a thousand times over him being in a grave. She smiled, her heart calling to the deepest parts of him for recognition of what they once shared.

"I don't," he finally answered her.

If it were possible for a person to deflate like a balloon, that was exactly what Demarcus thought Duchess looked like after his answer. He felt bad for hurting her, but he had to be honest. He had no idea who she was.

Suddenly, he felt suffocated by everything he'd just learned. He felt suffocated by Duchess staring at him with those pleading eyes, wanting him to be someone he wasn't. He stood up and headed for the door. He had to get out of here. All of a sudden, it was hard for him to breathe.

"This some bullshit, Rico," he said, and he walked out of the room, ignoring Rico calling out for him to stop.

"Well, that didn't go how I'd hoped," Rico said after Demarcus left. He shook his head in frustration.

Duchess was too grateful Duke was alive to allow her heart to feel disappointment. That was OK, because she was as sure as she knew her name that his memory would have to return. She was going to make sure of that.

An hour later, Ford, the twins, Duchess, and Rico were seated in Rico's oversized living room, discussing what to do next, when a distinguished, dark-skinned man with salt and pepper hair was escorted into the room by two armed men.

Rico introduced the man to the group as Dr. Peña. The doctor was renowned throughout the Dominican Republic. He was board certified and licensed to practice in three different countries, yet he jumped whenever Rico called him.

He listened intently as everyone tried to explain Demarcus's memory loss.

"Hmmm," Dr. Peña said while scratching his chin. "I really wish I had the opportunity to examine him for myself."

"That's not gonna happen anytime soon," Rico said. "He won't listen to a word we say, so I know he's not gonna let you examine him."

"It's like more than memory loss," Duchess said. "Like he really believes he's this Demarcus guy."

"That hardly makes any sense," Dr. Peña said. "I understand certain trauma to the brain can cause memory loss, but Duke should have fully recovered from that by now. His memory loss should have been a short-term thing."

"Told y'all," Gunz said with a satisfied grin on his face. He popped an invisible collar. "I be knowing."

"Unless..." Dr. Peña continued, "someone is influencing him."

"Influencing him?" Ford asked. "What'chu mean by that?"

"You said Duke's brain went without oxygen for a long amount of time, which caused the brain damage. That would definitely cause memory loss, but that memory loss should have been temporary unless someone with a high level of influence over him has convinced him he's in fact Demarcus and never was Duke. If that's the case, which I really hope it isn't, then Duke is in for a long fight of recovery."

"Shit!" Rico exclaimed, shocking everyone in the room. "My fuckin' cousin."

Everyone in the room stared at him, fully expecting smoke to come from his nostrils because he was that pissed off.

"Your cousin?" Dr. Peña asked.

"His wife," Rico clarified before Ford could stop him this time.

Rico's words took a moment to register before they settled deep into Duchess's soul. She should have been numb to pain by now, but the wounds that had taken so long to heal came splitting back open, causing her to wince. Duke had married someone else? Her heart felt like Rico had physically reached into her chest and pulled it out.

"My cousin claimed he was her boyfriend who had some boating accident that caused him to lose his memory. Ever since he came home from the hospital, he's been with her. She's been with him forever now, feeding him God knows what bullshit stories," Rico said.

"Oh no," Dr. Peña said. "Your cousin is playing a very dangerous game with this man's life. He may not remember who he is now, but the day will come when all of his memories *will* return. I feel sorry for her when that day comes, because those memories will replace any memories that he has made with her. When Duke returns, he will completely erase Demarcus."

Duchess gasped. Ford's eyes bucked, and the twins gaped at one another.

"Wait, what does that mean?" Rico asked, even though he was sure he already understood.

"When Duke's memories return, it will be like doing a factory reset on a cell phone. He will not remember ever being Demarcus," Dr. Peña said.

So all hope wasn't lost after all. Duchess felt a revival of her optimism at Dr. Peña's words. Duke *was* coming back. Everything was going to work out in their favor.

"Do you know how long that will take to happen?" she asked the doctor.

"I cannot say for sure," Dr. Peña said. "It could be next week, or it could be next year."

"Next year!" Ford jumped out of the chair he sat on. There was no way in hell he could let his brother lay up with some lying ass broad for a whole year, thinking he was someone else.

"I'm sorry. I cannot say for sure. But what I can say is the sooner you get him away from this person that is creating the fake memories fostering his false identity, the better the chances of Duke remembering who he truly is," Dr. Peña said.

"Say less!" Ford said, anger pumping throughout the blood in his veins. "Let me go kill that bitch tonight."

Rico shook his head. What Auri did was beyond wrong, but he couldn't sign off on her death certificate. She was family, so that made her untouchable. "I'm sorry, Ford. I can't let you do that."

"Let me?" Ford was seconds away from pulling his gun on Rico again. He was down for whatever when it came to his brother, so there was no way he was going to let Rico keep him from getting at the bitch responsible for Duke believing he was somebody else.

"She has a son," Rico said. "*They* have a son."

The impact of his words hit everyone in the room at the same time, at different levels of shock.

Duchess cried out in alarm. This was becoming too much for her to deal with. When she hopped on the plane this morning, she'd fully expected to have her man back. Now she was faced with a new reality. Duke was now Demarcus, a married man with a son, and no memory of Duchess whatsoever.

Hearing his brother had a son did little to douse the murderous rage Ford felt for Auri. He wanted Auri dead for what she'd done to his brother. She had him walking around here thinking he was someone else for a whole year while the whole city of Dallas mourned Duke. The bitch had to die, and Ford didn't give a fuck who she was related to.

Period.

CHAPTER FIVE

It didn't matter how many times Billie heard Duchess explain it, she still didn't understand how any of this happened. Duke was alive and living in the Dominican Republic with another woman. He had no memory of ever being Duke. Billie couldn't understand any of it, but her friend needed her right now. So she didn't ask any questions about the tour with Leela Lennox that Duchess had seemed to forget all about, or about Brian, who'd called Billie at least three times already for an update on Duchess. For whatever reason, Duchess hadn't taken any of his calls, so he looked to Billie for the answers only Duchess could provide.

All Billie could do was shake her head as she thought about the crazy turn things had taken. She stirred sugar into her coffee as she waited for her companion, who was over fifteen minutes late, to join her at the restaurant.

Jerrika hopped out of her brand-new Bentley coupe and tossed her blonde weave over her shoulders. Her oversized designer sunglasses hid the disdain in her eyes. There were a thousand things she'd rather be doing right now than meeting Billie. She was over her friendship with Billie and Duchess. She'd completely outgrown those broke hoes. These days, she couldn't remember why she ever fucked with them.

She entered the restaurant and knew immediately that she wouldn't be staying long. She hadn't eaten in this kind of hole-in-the-wall establishment in forever. If her car wasn't so well known around Dallas, she would have been afraid to even park it outside this place. Everyone knew who the fuck she was and who she belonged to, so she was good in any hood.

Billie's face lit up when she saw Jerrika walk through the door. Even though Jerrika had been on some bullshit lately, she had to admit she missed her girl. She missed the days when she, Duchess, and Jerrika used to hang out. These days, it was like they were strangers.

"Hey, Jerrika," Billie said as she went to hug her. She was taken aback by the coldness in Jerrika but decided not to say anything.

Jerrika sat down at the booth and didn't bother taking her sunglasses off. She didn't plan on staying here longer than five minutes to hear what was so important that Billie couldn't have told her over the phone.

"What's up, Billie? What's going on?"

"You gonna order something?" Billie asked, remembering how this used to be their spot after the club when they were all drunk as hell.

"Hell naw. I ain't gonna eat none of this shit." Jerrika curled her face up at the fact that Billie would even suggest she eat something out of this place. She wasn't sure why the health department hadn't shut it down yet.

Billie wanted to call Jerrika out on her stank ass attitude but decided against it. This wasn't the time or place. "Anyway, how's Shai?"

"He's good," Jerrika said while staring at her nails. She planned on leaving there and going to her new nail spot in Uptown, so she really hoped Billie didn't expect her to sit and play twenty-one questions all day.

Billie waited for Jerrika to ask how she was doing or even ask about Duchess, but when it became obviously clear that Jerrika had no intentions on doing so, she decided to get straight to the reason she'd asked Jerrika to meet her in the first place.

She took a deep breath. "I don't know if you knew it or not, but Duchess won a chance to go on tour with Leela Lennox. She was supposed to fly out yesterday. You know that's been her dream forever, to be a singer."

Jerrika sucked her teeth. She knew damn well Billie hadn't asked her to come here to tell her about some shit like that! Jerrika couldn't have cared less if someone paid her to do so. The last thing she wanted to hear was how Duchess was about to run off on tour with one of the biggest singers in the world. Envy tasted so bitter in her mouth as she thought about it.

It seemed like no matter how hard she tried to one up Duchess, she always came up swinging. Damn!

"Well, Duchess didn't get on that plane to go on tour with Leela," Billie said. She paused to sip her coffee.

"Why not?" Jerrika asked, finally curious to hear what Billie was getting at.

"Because she got a call from Ford. And Jerrika, you wouldn't believe what he told her."

Jerrika's already short patience had begun to wane. "Ford? What the hell did he want?" She hadn't heard Ford's name in what felt like years. She'd totally forgotten about the hot-headed boy.

"He found Duke."

Jerrika was glad her sunglasses were so huge that they covered most of her face. If it hadn't been for them, Billie would have surely read the facial expression that she couldn't hide. "Wha-what do you mean he found Duke?"

"Bitch, Duke is alive, living in the Dominican Republic." Billie laughed, but she wasn't sure why she was laughing. Maybe because of the sheer craziness of everything.

If Jerrika's stomach wasn't empty, she would have definitely thrown up right then and there. Of all the things for Billie to tell her, that was nowhere in the vicinity of what she'd imagined.

"What the fuck do you mean Duke is alive?"

Billie shrugged. "Rico never killed him, Jerrika! He's been alive this whole time and living in the Dominican Republic with some woman. And get this, he married the bitch and had a kid with her."

Jerrika couldn't have cared if Duke fathered an army's worth of kids. What she couldn't get past was the fact Duke was alive and well or the fact he hadn't tried to get back at Shai. None of what Billie was saying made any sense.

"That doesn't make sense, Billie. Why would Duke start a life in the DR and leave Duchess like that? Why would he let all of us think he was dead?"

"Oh, get this. He lost his memory. He has no idea he's Duke. He thinks he's somebody else. Duchess said he looked her right in the face and didn't blink or bat an eye."

Jerrika's heart raced so fast toward heart attack territory that she had to clench and unclench her fist to release the tension. "Oh my God."

"I know, right! I'm flying down there tomorrow to be with Duchess. You know she's tripping the fuck out. I really think you should come too. I know we all haven't been as tight as we used to be, but Duch could really use both of us right now."

Jerrika didn't know what to say. She only thought about was how fast she was going to call Shai and curse him completely out. He really fucked this one up! Was there anything he could do right? He couldn't even run the streets properly. If it wasn't for Jerrika, they wouldn't even have a plug right now. If it wasn't for her, niggas wouldn't even fear Shai. There had been several occasions where she had to send goons out on Shai's behalf to handle competing niggas itching to be the next King of Dallas.

"Shit," Jerrika said, thinking aloud.

"Girl, I know. It's crazy, huh."

"Crazy as hell." She bit down on her lip so hard, it began to bleed. "I'll go with you, Billie. You're right. Duchess needs both of us right now."

Billie smiled. She wasn't sure but was glad that for once Jerrika would come through.

Jerrika's mind raced. She was going to the DR, but it didn't have shit to do with looking out for Duchess. She had to see Duke with her own eyes to believe this amnesia bullshit. Whether he was faking or not, Jerrika planned on finishing what her sorry ass nigga couldn't. She would kill Duke, once and for all, to secure the throne she happily sat on now. For good measure, she would put Ford in the grave next to him, since he was out there discovering shit like he was Christopher Columbus.

Hell, who knew; maybe it was time to get rid of Duchess for good too.

CHAPTER SIX

Demarcus walked into the home that he shared with his wife, just like he did every other night, but this night, the enthusiasm to see her wasn't there. His mind was still reeling from what happened at Rico's house. No matter how hard he tried, he couldn't get Duchess's face out of his head. He didn't remember her, but he couldn't shake the way she reacted toward him.

"Daddy's home!" Auri called out as she met Demarcus in the foyer. She had Levi on her hip and a large smile on her face. The smile evaporated when she leaned in for a kiss and Demarcus pulled away.

"What's wrong?" she asked, immediately concerned. It wasn't like Demarcus to bring his work issues home with him.

For hours, Demarcus tried to figure out how he'd approach Auri, but now that he was face-to-face with her, all that preparation shit was out the window. He was confused and angry as hell. The only thing keeping him from slapping the shit out of her was the sweet smile on his baby boy's face. He reached for his son and walked past Auri.

"Uh, hello?" Auri was on his heels. She followed him and stood directly in front of him once he'd sat on the couch. "What, am I invisible or something?"

"Nah, you ain't invisible," Demarcus said, "but you are a liar."

Auri froze. Fear instantly coated her throat, making it impossible for her to speak. Was her worst fear coming to fruition?

Had Demarcus gotten his memories back? She was so afraid that she began trembling right in front of him.

"You ain't gotta be scared, Auri. I ain't gonna put my hands on you, even though I should." Demarcus returned his attention to his son, who giggled as he tickled him.

"What ha-ha-happened?" Auri stuttered.

"Rico had some broad at the house today. As soon as she laid eyes on me, she freaked the fuck out, calling me Duke and shit, just like the lil' nigga from the other night. I told Rico and the chick that they were out their minds 'cause my name ain't no Duke. Right, Auri?"

Demarcus watched Auri's reaction closely. The fear on Auri's face was so palpable that if he hadn't known for sure before, he knew now. She'd lied to him. His entire life here with her had been one big fucking lie.

Anger, confusion, and then more anger hit him with such force that he had to put distance between himself and Auri out of fear that he would really hurt her. He set Levi inside his playpen and then tried to settle the anger threatening to erupt inside of him.

"Demarcus, I can explain." Auri knelt in front of him. She cried as she tried to think fast. Never in a million years had she expected this to happen. What was with all the people from Demarcus's past popping up? For God's sake, they'd left him in a coma for months! Now they were here to ruin everything she'd worked so hard for. And her cousin, Rico, had a hand in it? What the fuck? She thought blood was thicker than water!

"Well, you better start explaining," Demarcus said. His voice was flat but at the same time threatening.

Auri had seen firsthand just how fast and explosive Demarcus's temper could be and she in no way wanted to experience that again, especially if his anger was directed toward her.

She thought fast and talked even faster.

"Demarcus, I never intentionally meant to lie to you," she said. "I swear to God, when I came to that hospital, I didn't go there trying to deceive you. It's just that... you didn't have anyone. You didn't know who you were, and the doctor was pushing you off on me. I couldn't just leave you there. I just couldn't."

"So you lied to me and led me to believe I'm someone that you knew damn well I wasn't!" Demarcus jumped up from the couch. Red hot anger pulsed through his body until it felt like he was on fire.

"I'm sorry!" Auri cried out. She cried so hard that she'd begun to hyperventilate.

Demarcus stared down at the woman he'd married. The woman who'd given him a son. The woman he loved. He didn't move to comfort her because, in this very moment, she wasn't any of those things to him. She was a bitch that had stolen the chance for him to remember who he really was.

He swept his son up and headed to the front door. He had to get as far away from Auri as possible. He was afraid of what he'd do if he stayed even a second longer.

Auri's eyes were red and swollen from crying for so long. She looked at the time on the microwave for what felt like the hundredth time. It'd been almost five hours since Demarcus left with Levi, and she was worried sick. He sent all of her calls to voicemail, so she had no idea where he was or if he was even coming back home. Her fear was irrational, but she feared he'd run back to America with Levi and she'd never see either of them again.

TARA ELLIS

She'd played a dangerous game, and she was reaping what she'd sown in the worst way. Just when she thought she'd finally gotten something good out of this shitty world, it took everything and more back from her. She felt like she would die. In fact, if Demarcus wasn't going to come back to her, she wanted to die.

She absolutely could not go back to her old life, not after experiencing real joy and happiness in the arms of Demarcus. Sure, she'd lied and plotted in the beginning of their relationship, but now they were a family. They were married and had a son. That couldn't be something he'd easily throw away, right?

Well, she wasn't about to wait around and find out. She got up from the couch and grabbed her car keys. Things were fucked up, but she was going to fix everything.

First thing first, she needed a gun, and she knew exactly where to go to get one.

CHAPTER SEVEN

Duchess wasn't in the mood for company. She thought she'd made that clear to Ford when he'd dropped her off at her hotel earlier. Obviously, she hadn't, because someone was knocking on her hotel door.

She pulled herself from the bed and wrapped the robe tighter around her body. She didn't care how she looked. Her eyes were bloodshot and puffy, her hair was all over her head, and her lips were dry and chapped.

She opened the door and almost stumbled backward because it wasn't Ford and the twins.

It was Duke. No, Demarcus.

"Uh, hi," she said.

"Can I come in?" he asked.

"Sure. Of course." She stepped aside and let him enter her room. When his back was to her, she ran her fingers through her unruly hair, trying to tame it.

"Ford told me where to find you," he said. He sat at the table in the middle of the suite. He kept folding and unfolding his hands, obviously nervous and uneasy.

Damn, Ford could have at least given me a heads up, Duchess thought. She didn't dwell on that though because, right now, Demarcus had all her attention.

It was wild to be face-to-face with the man she thought she'd buried. It was crazy to be able to talk to him again, to get that kind of second chance, even if he no longer could pick her face out of a crowd of people.

"This is crazy as hell to me," Demarcus said. He didn't know how to voice what he felt—confusion, betrayal, anger, and rage all wrapped together.

"I know," Duchess said. She stuffed her hands into the pockets of her robe because they begged to reach out and touch him.

"How am I supposed to remember who I used to be?"

"I can help you. That's why I'm here, Duke."

Demarcus flinched at the name. He knew it was his real name, but he didn't like being called it. It was only a reminder that something was wrong with him, a stabbing reminder that he couldn't even remember his own name.

"Don't call me that!" he snapped.

Duchess took a couple of steps back at the sharpness of his tone. Demarcus definitely wasn't Duke. Duke never spoke to her so sharply.

Demarcus looked up from his hands and into her dark brown eyes. There was something that connected with him. This woman was a stranger to him, but he could tell she loved him. Deeply. He regretted snapping at her like that. He was mad at Auri but taking his anger out on Duchess. He sighed and tried to relax. He forced a smile.

Duchess sucked in as much air as her lungs could take. She couldn't pull her eyes away from the dimples in his cheeks. Those dimples had always had the power to melt her insides. God, how she'd missed him.

Demarcus couldn't help but notice the way Duchess stared at him. Auri never looked at him that way. It had him wanting to know what kind of man Duke was for Duchess to love him this way. "Tell me about Duke," he said.

"Wow," Duchess said. Where should she begin? She had a thousand stories she could tell Demarcus in a thousand different ways. She didn't know where to start, so she decided to start at the beginning.

Jerrika handed her driver five one hundred-dollar bills as promised.

"You say it's that one?" She pointed to the largest house on the beach.

"Yes. That's where Demarcus and his family lives," the driver said nervously. He didn't have any business bringing this American woman to Demarcus's home, but the lure of five hundred American dollars was something he couldn't resist. Besides, what kind of danger could this prim and proper woman pose to a man as dangerous as Demarcus?

"Thanks," Jerrika said before getting out of the car.

She'd told Billie she would fly out with her, but she never planned on doing that. She had to get on the first thing smoking to the DR. She had to clean up Shai's mess before it had a chance to ruin everything she'd worked for.

She flew out without even telling Shai where or why she was going out of town. As of right now, the only person in Dallas that knew Duke was still alive was Billie, and Jerrika wanted to keep it that way. She didn't think Shai would tell anyone, but she wasn't taking any chances with his ass. He was beyond a fuck up.

Armed with what little information Billie had given her, Jerrika caught the first flight out of Dallas. Flying to the DR was only half the issue. She feared it would take days, if not weeks, to locate Duke, but all it took was one mention of the name Billie said Duke was going by: Demarcus.

The first person Jerrika had asked for information about a Black guy named Demarcus knew just who she was talking about. Duke had obviously made a name for himself down here in a short amount of time. Wasn't that just like Duke? The Duke of Dallas had quickly become the fucking Duke of the Dominican Republic. Jerrika was disgusted.

She wasn't sure if she believed this memory loss, amnesia bullshit. She had to see it with her own eyes to believe it. That's why she was here—at Duke's door. She would be able to immediately tell from his reaction if he was faking it or not.

Jerrika wasn't a fool though. She knew better than to show up to Duke's home unarmed. If he was faking it like she suspected, she would put a bullet between his eyes. She had the element of surprise on her side. Duke had no idea she was here.

Jerrika was glad she'd opted for Jordans instead of Louboutins as she ran across the street and onto the beach. Duke's house was the biggest and envy inducing. Jerrika couldn't believe he actually lived here! How did he manage to come up like this in just a year and a half? How was he this paid?

Nerves found their way into the pit of Jerrika's stomach. She wasn't sure what she was about to find on the other side of this door, but she was prepared to shoot first and ask questions later.

Demarcus listened intently as Duchess spoke. He laughed when she laughed, and his heart went out to her when she cried. He studied everything about her from the way she talked with her hands to the way she pulled her hair behind her ear when she became nervous. No, he didn't remember her, but he could see how he'd once loved her. She was kind and compassionate. She told him their love story with such passion that Demarcus wondered how it was even possible for him to forget a bond so unbreakable, a bond that seemed bulletproof.

"And that's why I hopped on a plane. I had to see you," Duchess said, finally at the end of the story. She didn't know how long she'd been talking, but her mouth was dry, and her eyes were wet.

"Damn," was all Demarcus could say after Duchess finished.

"I know," she said, wiping at her eyes. She was so tired of crying. When it came to Duke, that seemed like all she did.

Demarcus sat back and let everything she'd said sink into his soul. He wished he could remember just one of the things Duchess had told him. He wished Duke felt similar to him, but it was like hearing her talk about a stranger. The only thing he felt he had in common with Duke was the way they made money.

"You still don't remember anything?" Duchess asked, almost holding her breath in anticipation.

Demarcus shook his head. Duchess's shoulders fell, but she refused to become discouraged. Demarcus felt like it was only fair for him to now tell Duchess about Auri, how he met her, and how she'd deceived him into believing he was Demarcus.

"My first memory starts seventeen months ago," he said, and it was hard to keep the defeat from overtaking his voice. "You have all these memories of our time together, and I can't remember any of it. I don't remember ever living in the States. I only remember being here."

Duchess was silent as Demarcus told her how he woke up in a hospital room with no memory of how he got there. Her eyes widened when he told her he'd been shot twice, almost drowned, and was in a coma for weeks. He told her how Auri had come to the hospital and claimed him a day before he was going to be kicked out. How she fed him a bowl of lies of their past. How stupid he felt for eagerly eating them all while grateful to be told anything about a past he could no longer remember, only now to find out it was all bullshit.

"We can get you some help. We talked to a doctor. He said we need to get you away from the person that's influencing you in order for your real memories to come back," Duchess said. She didn't think it was possible to hate anyone more than she'd hated Rico, but this Auri chick took the cake. Duchess wanted just ten minutes alone in a room with her. She'd stolen the life that was supposed to be hers. She was supposed to be Duke's wife, the mother of his first child.

Demarcus thought about what Duchess had just said. Could he up and leave Auri? He was beyond pissed off at her and had no intention of being with her after what she'd done to him, but at the same time, Auri was all he knew. All the things he remembered included her. She was his wife and the only woman he could remember loving.

She'd put him in a fucked-up position, but if she hadn't rescued him from that hospital, where would he be right now? Where were Duchess and Ford when he needed them the most? They were nowhere to be found! Auri was there when he had no one.

And that was the very reason he could never hate her.

Jerrika knocked on the door and impatiently tapped her foot as she waited for someone to answer it.

Time seemed to move at a snail's pace before the door finally swung open.

Auri had hoped Demarcus had lost his key and was the one at the door knocking. She was immediately disappointed to see some Black bitch standing there with a scowl on her face.

"Who are you?" Auri asked, not trying to hide the contempt in her voice. She wasn't in the mood for whatever this woman was here for. It was past nine o'clock at night, so she hoped she wasn't here trying to sell her some shit, or Auri was going to go the fuck off.

"I'm looking for Duke," Jerrika said before giving Auri the once over. Was this the woman he'd married? She was pretty enough but looked nothing like Duchess. Even though Jerrika held animosity in her heart for Duchess, she had to admit this bitch didn't have shit on her.

Heat rose in Auri's chest. She had some nerve! Was this the same woman Rico had over his house and introduced to Demarcus? How dare she come to her door with the bullshit! Auri was seconds away from going completely off.

"Or Demarcus," Jerrika added. "Whatever he's calling himself these days."

"Look, bitch," Auri growled, "I don't know what kinda drugs you're on, but if you don't get off my step with that bullshit, I'm gonna kic—"

"I'm not your enemy," Jerrika interrupted. She could almost feel the anger radiating off this chick, but she didn't know why it was directed toward her.

"What do you want?" Auri snapped.

"Can I come in?"

"No the hell you cannot!"

"Trust me, you want to hear what I have to say."

Auri's mouth snapped close. She wasn't sure why she did it, but she stepped aside and invited the strange woman into her home.

Jerrika admired the house as she walked inside. Of course it was nice. Duke never half did anything, so why would he switch up in his double life?

"Follow me," Auri said as she walked into the living room. She sat down and invited the woman to do the same. "You have five minutes so get to the point. Fast."

"I knew Duke before he became Demarcus," Jerrika said. "I don't know how or why he became Demarcus. That's why I'm here. I was hoping to talk to him."

"That's never going to fucking happen!" Auri shouted.

Jerrika held both of her hands in the air. "Look, I don't know what your problem is, but you really need to chill the fuck out."

"Don't come into my house telling me to chill out! You people left Demarcus here for a year and a half, and then you suddenly pop up and try to rip him from my life! We're married," Auri said while holding up her left hand so Jerrika could see her wedding band, "and we have a child. A son! I'm not going to sit around and let you people steal that from me."

Realization hit Jerrika in the middle of Auri's rant. She sat back and smiled. Oh, this was good. This was even better than her original plan.

"I'm not sure who you're referring to when you say you people, but I can assure you that I'm not trying to steal Demarcus from you. In fact, it will be in my best interest if he never returns to Dallas."

Auri wiped at her eyes and gawked at Jerrika. "Wait, what? What are you talking about?"

"I heard about Demarcus's memory loss, and I came here

to see if it was true."

"It's true," Auri said.

"Good," Jerrika said. She grinned. No wonder Duke hadn't returned to Dallas to get revenge. He didn't remember who tried to kill him.

"And why the fuck is that good?" Auri asked.

"Because like I said, it's in my best interest that Demarcus doesn't remember ever being Duke and that he stays here with you and your son."

Jerrika had Auri's full attention now. "Who are you?"

"My name is Jerrika, and I used to be friends with Demarcus's fiancée."

"So why don't you want him to get his memory back or go back home to your friend?"

"Like I said, I *used* to be friends with her."

Auri narrowed her eyes at Jerrika. She couldn't get this chick's angle. She knew she couldn't trust her, but something about the way she stared at Auri made her believe her. For some reason, she truly didn't want Demarcus to remember who he really was.

That reason didn't concern Auri. In fact, she didn't want to know the reason. When she stared at Jerrika, she saw her for who she really was, an ally.

"OK, Jerrika. It's nice to meet you." Auri stuck her hand out for Jerrika to shake. "I'm Auri, Demarcus's wife." For the first time since Jerrika showed up at her door, Auri smiled. "Now, let's talk about how we're going to keep Demarcus in the Dominican Republic for good."

Jerrika smiled back at Auri. "First thing's first, we need to get rid of his brother and fiancée."

"Sounds like a plan," Auri said. She'd already planned on somehow doing that anyway, so now that she had someone who wanted the same thing just as bad, Demarcus's brother and old fiancée were as good as dead.

CHAPTER EIGHT

Brian wanted to throw his phone across the room. He'd lost count of the times he'd called Duchess. All of his calls had gone unanswered. At first, his texts were being left on read; now she was no longer even reading them.

He was going out of his mind, worrying about what the fuck was going on in the Dominican Republic between Duchess and her ex. He thought it was hard competing with a ghost, but competing with a man who'd returned from the dead? That was a losing game, and he knew it.

In spite of knowing that, he wasn't about to give up so easily. He loved Duchess, and she was on the verge of falling for him until Duke re-emerged. How the fuck did that even happen? He couldn't get in touch with Duchess for answers, and Billie had next to none.

At least Billie took his calls. He called her again. He knew it was too early in the morning to be calling someone, but right now, he didn't give a fuck.

"Hello?" Billie sounded wide awake.

"Billie? Have you heard from her?"

Billie heard the distress in Brian's voice, and her heart went out to him. Poor guy. He really had feelings for Duchess, and Billie wanted so bad to tell him it was best for him to move on with his life. Now that Duke was back, Brian might as well be dead because that's exactly what he was to Duchess.

"Yes, I've talked to her," Billie said.

Brian felt like Billie had kicked him in the stomach. Duchess was talking to her but ignoring him. Damn, is that how little she thought of him?

"I'm at the airport right now. My flight leaves in an hour. Jerrika was supposed to be coming, but I should have known she would flake. Bitch ain't worth shit, man."

"You're at Love Field airport?" Brian asked, hoping that she was because Love Field airport was only ten minutes from his house.

"Yeah, why?"

"I'm flying with you."

"Wait, what? Naw, Brian. I don't think that's a good idea."

"She won't talk to me, Billie. She won't call me back or respond to any of my texts, so what am I supposed to do?"

"Move on," Billie said flatly. She wanted to go easy on Brian's feelings, but he was talking crazy right now.

Brian huffed. "Move on? Just like that? Like this last year didn't mean shit? I'm sorry, Billie, but I can't do that. I love her."

Billie sighed. "I'm sorry, Brian. I don't really know what to tell you, but I know you popping up in the DR right now isn't a good idea. Duchess is dealing with a lot right now. I'm sure she'll hit you back when she can."

Brian wasn't listening to Billie anymore. He'd already thrown a couple of outfits into a bag and was now in his car headed straight to the airport.

He was going to get his girl by any means necessary.

Duchess woke up in Demarcus's arms. She wasn't sure how they'd fallen asleep together, but it wasn't a coincidence that they'd ended up in this position.

She lay there for a few minutes longer, savoring just how good it felt to be this close to Duke again. She pretended he wasn't Demarcus—he was Duke with all his memories. She relished in the fantasy, knowing one day soon it would be a reality. Dr. Peña may not have been able to put a timeline on it, but Duchess would wait forever if she had to.

Demarcus stirred behind her. Duchess quickly shut her eyes, pretending she was still asleep.

His eyes jolted open as soon as he realized where he was. He thought back to last night and was relieved when he remembered nothing happened between them. The last thing he wanted to do was give Duchess that kind of false hope. Whether she was a lying piece of shit or not, Auri was still his wife, and Demarcus wasn't going to cheat on her.

He climbed out of the bed, stretched, then searched for his cell phone and was surprised that it had battery life, with over ten missed calls from Auri and a couple from Rico. He glanced at Duchess, who lay in bed with her eyes closed.

He didn't have any memory of her that went past yesterday, but he felt a connection that he couldn't explain. It was possible his mind couldn't remember her, but his heart somehow did. He wanted to reach out to her, pull the stray pieces of her hair behind her ear. He wanted to feel the softness of her skin against his fingertips. He wanted to kiss her.

He shook his head as his phone vibrated in his hand. It was Auri. He rejected the call and walked into the bathroom. He closed the door behind him so he wouldn't wake Duchess.

After relieving his full bladder, he called Rico back.

"'Sup, Rico?" Demarcus's voice was rough, a clear indication of the day he'd had yesterday.

"What time are you coming by to pick up Levi?" Rico asked. He'd volunteered to keep him while Demarcus went to talk to Duchess, but he didn't think that would become an overnight thing. He couldn't blame Demarcus though; if it were him, he'd be deep inside the Black beauty.

"Damn, my fault, Rico. I'm on my way now."

Rico chuckled. "Long night, huh? Did the Duke and Duchess get reunited?"

"It ain't even like that," Demarcus said.

"Sure."

"Seriously, Rico. We just talked."

"Whatever you say."

Demarcus hung up with Rico and exited the bathroom. He was surprised to see Duchess sitting up in bed.

She smiled at him. "Good morning."

"Did I wake you?"

"No. I'm usually up earlier than this anyway. I work in a bakery, and I have to be there at the crack of dawn every day."

Demarcus nodded as if he understood. He grabbed his keys and wallet from the table.

Duchess frowned. "You're leaving?"

"Yeah. I gotta go pick up my son."

He didn't mean any harm by what he'd said, but his words sliced into her like a razorblade.

"Will I see you again today?"

"I don't know," he answered truthfully. He had a lot to sort out in his head.

Duchess swallowed the disappointment and refused to let it break her. She was staring at a man who shared the body of the man she loved but had to remind herself that he wasn't Duke... yet.

Until Duke's memories came back, she would have to give Demarcus time and space. That was easier said than done, especially when everything inside of her wanted to be with him.

"See you later," Demarcus said as he walked out of the hotel room. He wished he could say something, anything to ease the tension and awkwardness between them, but he couldn't. Everything was fucked up, and it was all Auri's fault.

Demarcus wasn't looking forward to being face-to-face with Auri again, but he couldn't delay the inevitable any longer. He stuck his key into the door, yet it swung open before he could even twist it.

Auri snatched Levi from Demarcus's arms. "How fuckin' dare you!" She understood he was pissed off at her, but he had no right to keep their son all night while ignoring her calls. She was worried sick.

Demarcus didn't say anything to her. He walked past her and into their master suite. Auri was on his heels.

"Where were you?" she demanded even though she feared the worst. Was that perfume she smelled on him?

Demarcus grabbed a pair of boxers from his underwear drawer and walked into their master bath. He craved a long, hot shower to relax the tension in his body.

"Were you laid up with some bitch? Huh, Demarcus? Answer me!"

"You mean my *real* fiancée? The woman I would have married if you hadn't lied to me about every damn thing? Is that who you're worried about, Auri?"

Auri refused to answer him; she refused to play this game with him. She didn't know if he was laid up with that Duchess bitch or not. If he had been, she was sure it was going to be the last time. Last night, she and Jerrika devised an almost perfect plan to eliminate their common enemies. Time wasn't on their side; they had to move fast because the more time Demarcus spent with Duchess and Ford, the larger the chance his memories would resurface. Auri would rather be dead than let that happen, which was why today they were putting their plan in motion.

She left their master bathroom and bounced Levi, who was becoming fussy, on her hip. "Sssh." She tried to comfort him while it was her heart that needed comforting the most. Her entire life was at stake and riding on this plan. Nothing could go wrong today.

She was in the living room playing with Levi when Demarcus reappeared fully dressed. He nearly took her breath away when she looked at him. Demarcus was so fine. The t-shirt he wore clung to every muscle in his arms for dear life. His shoulders were so broad and sexy. There was something about his aura that was commanding and had her captivated. She'd be damned if she lost this man.

"I gotta make a run, but I'll be back," he said, avoiding her eye contact. He couldn't even look her in the eye because he was still so pissed off at her. "When I get back, we got a lot to talk about."

"I know," she said.

"Like what's next for this family."

Auri frowned. "What is that supposed to mean?"

Demarcus scratched the side of his head. "I can't forgive and forget the bullshit, Auri. I don't think you even realize the gravity of what you've done."

"I know what I did," she protested, "but look at the beauty that came out of it!" She motioned between them and then at Levi. "This wasn't a mistake, Demarcus. This was supposed to happen."

"What gives you the right to play God with my life, Auri?"

She was speechless. She didn't know how to respond, so she sat there with her mouth open.

"I would say I want a divorce, but I'm pretty sure our marriage ain't even legal to begin with."

"Wait! No, Demarcus!"

"I'm gonna always look out for you 'cause you're Levi's mama. You ain't gonna ever have to worry about that."

"So what are you saying? You're leaving me?" The words almost got caught in Auri's throat.

"We'll talk about it when I get back," he said while shaking his head. He couldn't believe they were here. The thought of splitting up with Auri would have never even crossed his mind had Ford not showed up and completely turned his world upside down. He loved her, and he probably always would, but he could no longer be with her.

He grabbed his car keys and walked out of the house without giving Auri another glance.

This was the beginning of the end, the end of life as Auri knew it, unless the plan that she and Jerrika formulated worked.

For that very reason, it *had* to work.

CHAPTER NINE

Duchess couldn't ignore Brian any longer; he was downstairs in the lobby of her hotel. She should have talked to him before it came to this, but she found it easier to avoid him than to have this conversation. A lot of good that did because the nigga had literally hopped on a plane and followed Billie to the DR.

"Do you want me to go talk to the nigga?" Ford asked.

"Or let me go holla at him," Gunz said.

"No, that's alright. I got it," Duchess said, knowing full well if she sent either one of these hot heads downstairs to talk to Brian, he would be limping back to the States in some kind of cast.

"Weirdo ass nigga followed you down here?" Ford asked.

"We were kinda in a relationship. Since I got down here, I been ignoring him," Duchess tried to explain. "He wants some kinda answers, and I guess this is the only way he knew how to get them."

Ford shook his head. He didn't care what Duchess said. The nigga was weird, but to him, Duchess would always belong to Duke. He couldn't see her with anybody else. Plus, they had work to do. They needed to concentrate on getting Duke's memory back. Now, Duchess had an unnecessary distraction and it pissed him off.

"I'm sorry, Duch. I tried to stop him," Billie offered.

"It's cool. Lemme go talk to him." Duchess exited the room

and got on the elevator. As soon as she stepped off it, her eyes zeroed in on Brian. He gave her a weak smile that had her feeling guilty as hell for how she'd been playing him.

He walked up to her and hugged her. "Damn, it's good to see you, girl."

"Hey, Brian."

"So this what it takes for you to talk to me?" he asked once she pulled away from him. He took in her appearance. Was it possible for her to be even more beautiful than he remembered?

Her hair was pulled into a simple ponytail. Her face was bare of makeup, and she wore a simple, plain pink t-shirt and distressed jeans that hugged her hips and ass. To Brian, she looked more beautiful than he'd ever seen.

"I'm sorry, Brian. I really wasn't trying to ignore you. I was gonna call you back."

"When, Duchess? After you'd married your dead fiancé who just so happens to not be dead anymore?"

"I just needed time," she tried to explain. "Finding out Duke is alive was enough of a shock, but now I'm dealing with his memory loss. I just wasn't in the head space to talk to you."

Brian shook his head. "You could have told me that. Hell, you could have texted me that, and I would have understood. Knowing something, anything, would have been better than sitting at home wondering."

Duchess sighed. What did he want from her? She didn't know what else to tell him.

They walked over to the sitting area in the lobby. Brian sat a little too close to Duchess. What would have never bothered her now had her skin crawling. He was too needy, too clingy.

"So Duke is alive?" Brian asked.

"He is."

"What does that mean, Duchess? For you and me?"

She shrugged. "I'm not sure, Brian. Right now, I can't even think of a you and me. I hope you can understand that."

He didn't. He couldn't.

Duchess could read it all over his face. She sighed. "There can't be a you and me anymore… not with Duke being alive. I just can't. I love him, Brian. I've never stopped. You know that."

Yeah, he did, and it was the very reason he hated Duke so much. Ever since he met Duchess, he'd been competing with him for her heart. Well, today the competition finally ended. Duke had won, and there wasn't a thing Brian could do about it but bow out gracefully.

He took both of her hands inside his own and kissed them. "I understand, Duchess, and I wish you nothing but the best."

Duchess felt her heart twisting inside her chest. She'd just broken Brian's heart, but there wasn't any other way. She could never be with him. She belonged to Duke.

Brian stood and walked over to the check-in desk. He was there now, so he might as well stay a couple of days. He'd never been in the Dominican Republic before and knew after this trip, he'd never return. The Dominican Republic would always be the place he got his heart ripped out his chest and thrown to the ground.

Duchess felt heavy as she got back on the elevator. She felt like shit. Brian was a good guy, and he deserved better than what she could give him. She walked back to her room and interrupted what looked like a deep ass conversation inside.

"Duchess! Sit down and hear me out," Gunz said before she was even inside the room good.

"OK… What's up?"

"You said Demarcus told you he'd been shot twice before thrown in the ocean, right?" Gunz asked. His eyes were wide and animated.

Duchess nodded.

"Shai said he was below deck when he heard gunshots and when he went back up, Duke was nowhere to be found," Ford said, working out the scenario in his head. "That story never sat right with me."

"But it lines up with what Duke told Duchess last night," Tommy said.

"Which would make Rico the snake ass nigga that we thought he was!" Gunz yelled. He punched his fist into his open palm, mad he didn't take Rico out when he had the chance.

"But why would Rico want to kill Duke?" Billie asked. "And then later, start working with him, even making him his lieutenant?"

"Yeah, what would be Rico's motive?" Duchess asked, taking a seat. The wheels in her mind worked overtime.

"My point exactly," Ford said. "He didn't have a motive. He didn't try to kill Duke."

"Then who did?" Gunz asked, shaking his head. He had crazy love for Ford, but he couldn't understand why his nigga was being so gullible right now.

"Who had the most to gain from Duke's death?" Duchess asked, thinking aloud.

The room went silent. Then, her eyes flew up. She looked at everyone in the room, and they all wore identical expressions on their faces.

"Shai!" Ford and the twins said at the same time.

Silence fell upon the room as everyone digested the revelation.

"Wasn't Jerrika supposed to fly down here with you?" Duchess asked Billie. She didn't want to believe the crazy shit playing with her mind right now. "You don't think she told him Duke was still alive and that she was coming down here and he… hurt her?"

"He wouldn't hurt Jerrika," Billie said, even though she didn't even believe it.

"Shiiiiit," Gunz said. "A snake don't care who it bite. If he crossed Duke, he'd definitely cross Jerrika's ass."

Ford expelled a deep breath. Anger had his chest rising and falling at a rapid speed. If what he thought was true, Shai had fucked all of them. "I'm gonna kill him," he said.

"Wait, no! You don't even know if it's true," Billie tried to reason. "Y'all just speculating right now."

"Shit makes sense though, Billie," Tommy said, shaking his head. Never would he have thought Shai would be so treacherous.

"First thing's first, we gotta get Duke's memory back, then we get our asses back to Dallas," Ford said, "and prepare for war."

"It's definitely gonna be a war," Billie said. "GMB runs Dallas, and they're loyal to Shai."

"Off the strength of Duke!" Ford yelled. "What you think the streets gonna do when they find out Duke ain't dead? That his right hand tried to murk him?"

Billie sat in silence.

"It's over for Shai's punk ass," Ford said, fuming. "As soon as I touch down in Dallas, it's over for that pussy." Fury made him scream and punch a hole straight through the wall of the hotel room. Shai was going to pay for all of this shit. He turned their lives upside down, for what? Greed?

Ford thought he hated Rico, thought he was going to give

Rico a slow death, but what he'd planned for Rico seemed merciful in comparison to what he was going to do to Shai. Shai had once been family; his betrayal would cost him his life.

Ford's mind was made, and there wasn't anything anyone in the room could say to change it.

Neither Auri or Jerrika had ever shot a gun in their lives, yet both of them were convinced they could kill Ford, who had perfect aim with his eyes closed.

Common sense was a luxury that neither one of them could afford right now. They both needed Ford dead, and it was up to them to make it happen. They ran through the plan one more time.

"You ready?" Jerrika asked.

"As ready as I'm gonna be," Auri said, remembering what Demarcus said before he left the house this morning. Every time she had second thoughts, she remembered, and it gave her the courage she needed to commit her first murder.

"Let's do this shit then!" Jerrika yelled. She was hype and drunk off adrenaline.

Auri started the rental car, and Jerrika hopped in the back seat. When they made it to their destination, they parked, turned the lights off, and waited.

Ford and the twins walked to the small colmado down

the street from their apartment. It was a small store that rarely had the things they needed but kept them from always having to travel into the city.

Tommy and Gunz waited outside while Ford ran inside and scooped up the things they needed.

"Good afternoon." The store owner greeted Ford.

"How you doing, Higuel?" Ford set his backpack on the counter before walking down the aisle to select what he'd come for. When he first started coming to this shop, he felt some way about having to leave his bag with the store owner, but after seeing the store owner make the same request of everybody, Ford didn't trip.

He grabbed what he needed and paid for them. As soon as he walked out of the store, the owner picked up his phone and dialed the number that had been given to him earlier today.

"He just left," he said. A part of him felt guilty. Over time, he'd gotten to know Ford and actually liked the young kid. These days, it was harder and harder to make ends meet, so he had to do what he had to do to take care of his family.

Ford and the twins were so wrapped up in their conversation that they didn't notice the strange car creeping down the small dirt road at a slow pace.

Jerrika didn't expect to see the twins. Their presence put a big ass wrench in the plan. She had half the mind to tell Auri to abort the plan. The odds were against them now. Jerrica took too long to make that call, because Auri slowly let her car window down just enough to stick her gun out. She squeezed the trigger while bringing the car to a complete stop. Due to her inexperience with a gun, her aim was trash and missed Ford completely.

Ford immediately ducked and tried to take cover while pulling his own gun from his backpack. Unlike Auri, his aim was precise.

He squeezed the trigger, prepared to return fire, but his gun clicked. The clip was empty! What the fuck? Ford looked at the twins as they ran and scrambled to take cover. Ford glared at his useless gun. Since when did he leave the house without a loaded gun? He knew full well he'd never make that kind of mistake. That kind of mistake could cost a man his life, and it looked like it was going to do just that right now.

After seeing Auri successfully cause Ford and the twins to take off running, Jerrika pulled her own gun and shot in the same direction that Auri let her bullets fly. She had no idea if they were actually hitting something, but the amount of shots that were being let off meant at least one had to hit.

Jerrika's gun clicked. Did that mean she was out of bullets? Or had her gun jammed? She had no idea, but she was scared as shit, especially once she noticed the twins had regained their composure and were now returning fire. Gunz, the bolder of the two, stepped out front for a better shot.

Auri screamed as the windows in her car exploded. She dropped the gun, which she didn't know what the hell she was doing with, and pressed her foot on the gas. She had to get the fuck out of there, but it was too late. She felt the first bullet and then the second. The pain was something she'd never felt before in her life. She screamed in pain as she drove recklessly out of the ran down neighborhood, cursing herself all the way. Who did she think she was? It was too late for regrets now. She was losing blood at a rapid rate, and her vision was doubling. She was dying.

She heard the sounds of tires screeching and metal colliding. The last thing she heard was the sound of Jerrika's screams in the back seat before everything went black.

CHAPTER TEN

Duchess returned from the hotel gift shop with a black dress that she wouldn't have worn under any other circumstances. Tonight, however, she didn't have a choice. She hadn't packed anything to wear on a date, so the dress would have to do.

A couple of hours earlier, she'd received a text message from Demarcus that almost made her heartbeat come to a complete stop.

Can I take you to dinner tonight?

Duchess had never responded to a text so fast in her life! She ran around her hotel suite, trying to doll herself up as if it were her first date with Duke. In a way, it felt exactly like that.

"Calm down!" Billie laughed. "You gonna have a panic attack if you don't chill out."

"I'm trying, Billie," Duchess said, "but I'm nervous as hell."

Billie tried to say something, but the sound of knocking on the door stopped her. Duchess sucked in air as Billie got up to answer the door.

She'd been told Duke was alive. She'd been told the story by both Duchess and Ford, but being face-to-face with him had Billie feeling like she was staring into the eyes of a ghost. "Duke?" she whispered before covering her mouth with her hand to smother the scream coming next.

Demarcus lifted an eyebrow. Who was this chick? Obviously, someone else from his past that he couldn't remember. He cleared his throat. "Uh, is Duchess ready?"

Duchess stepped in front of Billie, who still gaped at Duke with tears running down her face.

"Demarcus, this is Billie, my best friend," Duchess said. "Billie, this is Demarcus."

"Duke…" Billie whispered again.

"Uhh… it's nice to meet you, Billie…?" Demarcus said more as a question than a statement.

Billie shook her head as if that would make this entire scene less shocking.

"I'll call you later, girl," Duchess said before closing the door. She turned to Demarcus and smiled. "She just flew in this morning."

"She came to support you? That was real cool of her," Demarcus said.

They walked down the hall and caught the elevator to the first floor. They were silent as they walked to Demarcus's car. Duchess wished she could read his mind, while Demarcus wished he could remember her.

When they made it to Demarcus's favorite restaurant, even though there was a long wait, they were seated immediately. Duchess couldn't help but laugh. Things had changed, but some things were exactly the same. Duke was still a boss and respected by everyone he came into contact with.

After they ordered their food, Demarcus spoke. "I talked to Dr. Peña today. He seems to think I can get my memories back any day now."

"That's wonderful," Duchess said. "How do you feel about that?"

"Shit, I really don't know. All this time, that's all I ever wanted. But he told me when my memories return, it's gonna be like I just left you yesterday. Like, this last year never happened. I'm not gonna even remember my son's birth."

Duchess watched the change in Demarcus's face and saw that bothered him. She didn't know what to say. She had no idea how he felt about any of this.

"So, a part of me is like damn, do I really even wanna remember?" Demarcus said. "Then, the other part of me knows I can't continue to live my life like this." He paused before dropping the real bombshell. "I'm through with Auri though."

"You are?"

"Hell yeah. I can forgive and forget a lot of shit, but what she did was unforgivable." Just thinking about it gave Demarcus a bad taste in his mouth.

If Demarcus was leaving Auri, what did that mean for Duchess? Did that mean he was returning to America with her?

"I'm not saying I'm about to hop on the first plane back to Texas," he said, as if he could read the hope on her face.

"Eventually though?" Duchess had to know.

He looked into her eyes and couldn't bring himself to hurt her any more than he already had. "Eventually."

Duchess could have jumped up from the table and wrapped her arms around Demarcus at that very moment, but the sound of his cell phone ringing brought her back to her senses.

He frowned when he saw the unfamiliar number on his cell. He was about to reject it, but something told him to answer it.

"Yeah," he said.

Duchess watched his facial expression morph into something she'd never seen on Duke's face. He abruptly stood, almost knocking the entire table over.

"I'll be there in ten minutes," he said before ending the call.

"What's wrong?" Duchess asked.

"My wife... she's been in an accident. I gotta go."

His wife? Seconds earlier, he was talking about leaving her. Now, Auri was his wife again. Duchess stood. "OK, let's go. Let's get out of here."

Minutes later, they were speeding down the road toward the hospital. Demarcus didn't even attempt to park straight when they arrived. He barely shut the engine off, before he ran inside the hospital. Duchess would've had to bust into a full speed run to catch up with him.

"I'm here for Auri Jones," Demarcus told the first person he saw. "She was just admitted. She was in a car accident or something."

Duchess entered the hospital just as Demarcus was being led to the east wing of the hospital. She followed him, even though she was sure he'd completely forgotten she was there.

"Mr. Jones, your wife is in surgery right now," a doctor said before Demarcus could push his way into the room.

"Surgery?"

"Yes," the doctor said, his accent thick. "She was shot twice and has lost a lot of blood."

"Shot!" Demarcus's voice was so loud that it could be heard down the hall and almost to the west wing of the hospital. "You telling me somebody shot my fuckin' wife!"

"Calm down, sir." The doctor looked at Duchess for assistance, but she averted her eyes. "We're going to do everything in our power to save her life."

Demarcus grabbed the doctor by his collar and shoved him against the wall. "Oh, you better save her life, doc, or you're the one who's going to be in surgery next."

"Demarcus!" Duchess tried to grab him and pull him off the doctor, but it was pointless. Demarcus may not have remembered being Duke, but they both shared that same point of no return anger. Duchess had seen it a handful of times, and she'd always been the only one able to bring him back to sanity. Demarcus didn't know her, so her pleas for him to stop fell on deaf ears.

It took several nurses to pull Demarcus from the doctor who was almost too distraught to go back into surgery. Demarcus plopped down into one of the hard chairs in the waiting room. He buried his face in the palms of his hands.

Duchess was at a loss. She had no idea what to do or say to him.

"Duchess," he said, his voice almost too low to be heard. "Go home."

"Huh?"

"Go home," he repeated. "I'm needed here. My family needs me. I'm not going anywhere."

She could have protested, but what was the point. She walked off, pulled her cell phone out, and called Ford.

"Ford, come get me. Please. Come get me out of here."

"Where are you?" was all Ford asked. He heard the shakiness in Duchess's voice and knew it was taking everything inside of her to keep it together.

Demarcus was by Auri's side when she was wheeled out of surgery. He slept beside her bed with the same reoccurring thought running through his mind. Who was stupid enough to try and kill his wife?

"Demarcus?" Auri's voice was weak and low, but Demarcus heard it. His eyes snapped open.

"Auri? Baby, are you OK? How do you feel?"

"Like shit," she said as she struggled to sit up.

"Naw, chill out. Don't try and move. You just got out of surgery."

"Surgery?"

"You was shot, Auri. The bullets missed a major artery by six centimeters. Six fuckin' centimeters, Auri." The thought had Demarcus ready to go on a rampage. "Baby, do you have any idea who tried to kill you?"

Last night's events came flooding back to her head. She and Jerrika had tried to kill Ford, but the plan went awfully wrong. He'd gotten away, and she'd landed in the hospital.

"Ford," she said. "He tried to kill me, baby." She managed to form tears and pretended she was so scared that she trembled.

Demarcus's eyes bulged, and he stepped back from the bed. Ford? His brother? Why the fuck would he try him like that?

"What about the girl that was with me?" Auri asked. "Did she make it?"

Demarcus shook his head, bringing his thoughts back from the murderous lane they'd verged into. "What girl? You were by yourself, Auri. What are you talking about?"

She shook her head. "Oh, I guess I just got confused."

She had no idea what happened to Jerrika, but obviously, she'd survived and escaped before the ambulance arrived. Auri couldn't worry about her right now. She saw the wheels turning in Demarcus' head and wondered if she should add that Duchess was with Ford when he tried to kill her. Maybe that would be enough for Demarcus to turn his back on both of them for good.

"Demarcus, I'm so scared. What if he finds out that I didn't die? What if he comes back? I know it was wrong what I did to you, but I don't deserve to die for it."

"Ssssh," Demarcus said while rubbing her head to comfort her. "You ain't gotta worry about that nigga. I'm gon' handle his ass. You ain't gotta worry about that one at all."

Auri felt a mix of relief and satisfaction, but she couldn't relax just yet. She still needed to know. "Are you still gonna leave me?"

Demarcus shook his head. "Never. I ain't going nowhere, Auri."

She sat back and smiled. Checkmate. She'd won.

CHAPTER ELEVEN

It'd been two days since Duchess heard from Demarcus. All of a sudden, he was avoiding her. She couldn't stay in the Dominican Republic forever, waiting on him. She had a job back home and bills that weren't going to pay themselves. She'd walked away from the opportunity of a lifetime with Leela Lennox, all for what?

"I think it's time for all of us to leave the Dominican Republic," Billie said, knowing that was going to fall on deaf ears. "I don't think it's safe here for any of us anymore. I mean, listen, Ford. Somebody tried to kill y'all the other day!"

"Somebody? I know exactly who tried to get at us," Gunz growled.

Duchess looked at him. "Who?"

"Rico! Who else?" His face went stone hard. "I told y'all we couldn't trust him! The nigga tried to body Duke, and now he coming after us because we figured the shit out."

"Gunz, shut the fuck up!" Ford said. "One minute, you talking 'bout it was Shai who tried to kill Duke, then the next, it was Rico. You don't know what the fuck you talkin' about!"

Ford was beyond frustrated. Two days ago, someone had tried to kill them, but he couldn't figure out who. It had him suspicious of everybody. He hated being paranoid, but until he was able to put a face and name to the white Corolla that snuck up on them the other day, he had to keep looking over her shoulder.

Tommy laughed and Gunz shrugged. "I'm just saying."

"Well, I'm saying I'm getting the fuck outta here," Billie said. Her flight was leaving tomorrow. She wanted Duchess to come with her, but she knew she wouldn't.

Everyone froze when the sound of someone knocking at the door so hard it sounded like they were trying to kick it in. Ford pressed his finger to his lips and grabbed his pistol from the coffee table. He walked over to his door and peered through the peephole. He visibly relaxed when he saw it was Demarcus.

"It's cool," he looked over his shoulders and told the twins before opening the door. "It's just Demarcu—"

Demarcus grabbed Ford by his throat and slammed him against the wall before he could even finish his sentence. He ignored the screams of Billie and Duchess. He glared into Ford's eyes. "You tried to kill my wife, nigga? You that fuckin' stupid?"

Ford didn't know what Demarcus was talking about. Sure, he wanted to kill Auri and probably would eventually, but he hadn't had the chance yet. He struggled to speak against what felt like his windpipe crushing. "Say man, I don't know what the fuck you talkin' 'bout."

Ford struggled to pull Demarcus's hands from his throat, but the more he tried, the harder Demarcus squeezed.

"I'm gonna break ya fuckin' neck for that shit, lil' nigga," he growled. He saw red, and the only thing on his mind was revenge. Brother or not, Ford fucked up when he touched what belonged to him.

The sound of two hammers being cocked behind him made Demarcus freeze in place before slowly turning around to access the threat. The twins had guns trained on him, aim steady and unwavering.

"Let 'em go, big homie," Gunz ordered. "I don't wanna Swiss cheese ya ass 'cause I got real love for you, whether you

THE DUKE AND DUCHESS OF DALLAS 2

remember that or not. But if you don't let my nigga go right now, it's gonna look like the Fourth of July up in here."

Demarcus hesitated, but the crazy ass look in Gunz's eyes told him the little nigga wasn't bluffing. He reluctantly released Ford.

"What the fuck wrong with you?" Ford coughed out while trying to suck in the air he'd been deprived. He rubbed his neck while glowering up at Demarcus. It was taking everything in him not to go to blows with him. There were only so many passes he could give.

"Auri is in the hospital. She was shot twice Thursday night, and she said you was the shooter," Demarcus snarled.

"She a gotdamn lie!" Ford howled. "Thursday night, me and my niggas were ducking and dodging bullets our damn selves! I don't know what that lying ass bitch talkin' bout!"

Demarcus ignored everything Ford said. His voice was low and hostile. "Ya friends were here to save you this time. Next time, you won't be so lucky. Brother or not, you crossed the fuckin' line when you touched my wife."

Demarcus didn't wait for a reply. He walked out of the small apartment and stormed down the hall.

Duchess got up and chased after him. "Demarcus!"

He didn't turn around. He didn't want to see Duchess right now, or ever again, really. That was the main reason he hadn't returned any of her calls. She was someone from a past that he couldn't even remember, and he planned on leaving her there.

"Demarcus, wait!" Duchess caught up with him and grabbed him by his arm to stop him.

He snatched away from her. "Duchess, go back home! There's nothing here for you."

"You're here, Duke. So as long as you're here, that's where I'm gonna be."

"I'm not Duke! My name is Demarcus!"

"But you know that's not true."

"It doesn't really matter anymore, Duchess. I don't remember being Duke, and I may never remember that shit."

"Or you may wake up tomorrow and remember everything!"

"That's a chance that I'm just gonna have to take."

"What does that even mean? Come back home with me, Demarcus. Please. You'll never get your memory if you stay here. You need to come home."

"This is my home. This is the only home I've ever known, and I'm staying here."

Duchess felt herself die a little.

"I'm not Duke, and I don't even wanna remember being him. I'm Demarcus, and I have a wife and son here. My family is here, and I'm not taking off and leaving them for a life that's no longer mine."

Duchess stepped backward as if his words had physically slapped her in the face. "But you know the truth now. You know you're not Demarcus. You know you have a whole life back in Dallas. Are you saying that's not enough for you?"

He shook his head. "I'm sorry this had to happen to you, Duchess. I wish you still believed I was dead, because that's exactly what Duke is. He's dead, and you're gonna have to let him go, because I'm not him, and I never will never be."

"So that's it? You just gonna dismiss me like it's nothing?"

"It is nothing. To me, Duchess, it's nothing. I feel nothing for you."

He might as well have pulled out a gun and shot her in the heart, because his words killed her.

"Do you have any idea how fucked up that is? For you to stand there in Duke's body and say you feel nothing for me when I feel *everything* for you! I will always love you. You may not remember me, but I'll never be able to forget you."

Demarcus didn't know what to say. She was asking too much of him. Duchess wanted him to be someone he wasn't. Why couldn't she understand that he wasn't Duke?

He ran his hand down his face in frustration. "I'm not Duke."

"I know you're not! You're not even half the man he was!" Duchess spat the words, wishing they hurt as much as his had destroyed her.

"Go back home, Duchess. Get the fuck out of the Dominican Republic, and take your friends with you. Because I promise you if I ever see Ford again, I'm sending him back to Dallas in a body bag." And with that, Demarcus disappeared down the hall and out of Duchess's life for good.

CHAPTER TWELVE

"You sure you don't wanna come back home with us?" Duchess asked Ford for the hundredth time, wishing this would be the time he agreed. Demarcus's threat still rang in her ears. He would do his best to make good on that threat. She'd already lost Duke, so she didn't want to lose Ford too.

Ford hugged Duchess. "Nah. I'mma be alright, Duch. You ain't gotta worry 'bout me."

She gave him a weak smile before looking at the twins. "What about y'all?"

They looked at one another before looking at Duchess. "Now you know we gon' ride with our nigga," Gunz said with a grin.

"I know," she said with a sigh. "Well, take care of him for me, OK?" She hugged the twins, knowing they would ride to the ends of the earth for Ford. Their loyalty was unmatched.

"You already know," Tommy told her.

Duchess watched Billie walk over to check in their bags, and she fought back the urge to cry. She really didn't want to leave. She hadn't accomplished anything that she came here to do. She expected to return to Dallas with Duke. Yet once again, she was leaving the Dominican Republic with half of her heart.

"Be easy, Duch, OK?" Ford said. He was about to turn and walk away when she reached out and grabbed him.

She stared at him with watery eyes. She wanted to say

anything that would change his mind and convince him to get on that plane with her and Billie. Demarcus was out for blood, and Ford didn't seem to see the severity of the situation. She searched her brain for the right thing to say to get through to him.

It was a lost cause, because Ford's mind was made up, and there wasn't anything Duchess could say to change it. There was no way he could leave this country knowing his brother was still here believing he was someone else. No, Ford wouldn't return to Dallas until he had Duke back.

The real Duke.

He gave Duchess a final hug and walked out of the airport, knowing it wouldn't be the last time he saw her.

Duchess sighed, said a silent prayer for Ford's safety, and followed Billie to their flight's departure gate.

She almost dropped her bags when she saw who was also seated waiting for the same flight back to Dallas.

Brian.

She was immediately embarrassed. It was bad enough she was returning home without Duke, but she had to face the man she'd rejected for the man who had rejected her. She might as well have had pie on her face. She could see the questions dancing all around Brian's face. Where was Duke? Why was she leaving without him?

She sighed and decided to just get it over with. She sat next to Brian and was surprised when he placed his hand on top of hers and squeezed. "It's OK," he said. "I'm here for you, Duchess. Please don't push me away. I don't care how long it takes. I'll wait for you."

Duchess could have burst into tears, because that's exactly how she felt about Duke. She was willing to wait for however long it took for his memory to return, but he'd pushed her away. She wouldn't make the same mistake twice. This time, she would allow Brian to heal her broken heart.

Jerrika watched Demarcus enter the store. She'd been following him since the day her plan to kill Ford went to shit. She still didn't know if Auri had survived, and she didn't really give a fuck. That didn't change her plans one bit. Jerrika came to the Dominican Republic to go to war, eliminating every threat to the empire she and Shai had built in Dallas. Auri just so happened to be a casualty of war.

Jerrika entered the same store she watched Demarcus walk into. The store was large, so it took her a few minutes to locate him. As soon as she laid eyes on him, her heart rate increased. She didn't know for sure if he'd really lost his memory. She was only going off what Billie and Auri had told her. Going off hearsay was what landed her in this whole mess to begin with. She needed to see it for herself.

"Excuse me," Jerrika said with a girly giggle as she reached for the same canned good as Demarcus.

"You good," he said without even turning to look at her.

"You take it. It's the last one," she said.

Demarcus turned to look at her. "Naw. It's all yours."

Jerrika stared into his eyes, waiting for a flicker of recognition or a flash of anger. Waiting for something, anything.

Nothing.

Demarcus only stared back blankly.

That was all it took for Jerrika to be convinced. He must have really lost his memory or had some kind of brain damage.

Sure, he looked just like Duke, but this *wasn't* Duke. His mannerisms were off. He didn't carry himself like Duke once had. It was like someone else was trapped in Duke's body.

Jerrika had done her research and learned Demarcus had somehow worked his way up to being Rico's right-hand man. Killing him would be incredibly hard and risky. Was it even worth it, especially seeing as though he didn't even realize he was Duke? What danger could he possibly pose to her?

None.

She took the canned good and smiled at Demarcus. "Thank you."

On her way out of the store, she set the can down and smiled all the way to her car. She still needed to take care of Ford. Auri told her the more time Demarcus spent with Ford, the greater the chance his memory would return. So Ford had to go. Their plan may have gone terribly wrong, but Jerrika wasn't giving up that easily.

She hopped into her new rental car and used her GPS to direct her to the colmado near Ford's apartment.

As soon as she entered the small store, Higuel frowned. He'd hoped to never see Jerrika again. Their business was finished. He'd done his part, so why was she here now?

"Go away. I can't help you," he said.

"You sure about that?" Jerrika asked, pulling several hundred dollar bills out of her wallet and waving them in the air.

Higuel looked around at the three customers in his shop before narrowing his eyes at Jerrika. "Come to my office. We can talk in private there."

Jerrika smiled and followed the old man into the rear of the store. He unlocked the door to a small office and flipped on the light.

"Take a seat and wait right here. Let me take care of my customers."

"Hurry back now," Jerrika sang.

Five minutes later, after checking out the remaining customers, Higuel flipped the open sign to closed and met Jerrika in the back. He was apprehensive to what the young American woman wanted this time. The first time she came by, she'd asked him to do something that not only put his life in jeopardy but the lives of his family. He didn't care how much money she flashed around this time; he wouldn't do such a thing again.

"I cannot help you," he said.

Jerrika put her hand in the air. "I don't wanna hear that shit. I just paid you five grand, and I don't think I even got my money's worth."

"What! Do you know what Ford would have done to me if he caught me rumbling through his backpack?"

Jerrika shrugged. "That's not my concern."

Higuel pointed to the door. "Get out!"

Jerrika crossed her legs and sat back. "Look, I didn't come here to raise your blood pressure. I came to ask for another favor."

"I cannot help you anymore. Please. Just leave."

"Bitch! Stop whining and crying. Look, I paid you five grand, and the nigga still got away without a scratch!"

"That's not my problem. You told me to ensure he left here with an empty gun. I did that! I cannot involve myself any further."

"Oh, you will help me, or Ford will get an anonymous tip telling him how coincidental it was that the day he was shot at, his gun just so happened to be empty." Jerrika placed a finger on her chin. "Hmmm, could it have something to do with Higuel, the owner of the colmado who makes you leave your belongings with him at the register?"

Higuel sighed. He didn't know if Jerrika was bluffing, but he didn't want to take that kind of gamble with his life. He felt defeated. "What do you want me to do this time?"

Tommy looked over his shoulder twice before crossing the street. He pulled his hoodie down further over his head. His head was on a swivel just in case someone wanted to jump stupid again. He cursed under his breath that he had to walk to this store anyway. How Gunz let them run low on cigarillos was beyond him, and he was pissed he had to be the one to walk to the store. He wasn't as paranoid as Gunz, but his nerves were still bad. Until they figured out who had made the attempt on their lives, Tommy thought everyone was suspect.

When he made it to the colmado, he was surprised to see a closed sign in the window.

"What the hell, man?" he groaned. This was the closest store, and he really didn't feel like driving all the way into town for a pack of cigarillos. He pushed the door open, hoping Higuel had just forgotten to flip the sign over.

"Hello?" Tommy called out.

Higuel wasn't behind the register, so he looked up and down the aisles for the old man. Tommy was about to hop behind the counter and just take the damn cigarillos and leave the money on the counter, when he thought he heard voices in the back of the store. "Aye! Somebody back there?"

No response.

Tommy got a funny feeling in the pit of his stomach. Something told him to mind his damn business, turn around, and get the hell out of there. Tommy didn't listen to that tiny voice in his head. He grabbed the doorknob and turned it.

Higuel almost jumped out of his skin at the sudden appearance of Tommy. He immediately recognized him as one of the guys that hung out with Ford. Tears welled in his eyes. Had he come here to kill him for the stunt he pulled the other day?

"What the fuck?" Tommy said, his eyes wide as they went from Higuel to Jerrika. "Jerrika! What the fuck you doing here?"

Jerrika jumped to her feet. Her mind went blank as she struggled to come up with a plausible reason why she was not only in the Dominican Republic, but in a store that was on the same block where Ford lived, chopping it up with the owner.

Everything about the scene before him looked suspect as hell. The wheels in Tommy's head spun so fast that it didn't take long for him to put the picture together. Suddenly, it all made sense. The day someone got at them, they had just left this same store. Ford's gun was magically empty, and Ford never left home with an empty ass gun. Seeing Jerrika here put the missing pieces together. Turns out, Shai wasn't the only snake hiding in plain sight.

"Please! No, no, no," Higuel begged with both of his hands in the air.

Even if Tommy had been slow to figure things out, the fear on Higuel's face told it all. Without hesitation, Tommy pulled his Glock 40 and shot him in the forehead.

He turned to Jerrika and shook his head in disgust. "All this time, it was you and Shai. What part of the game is that, Jerrika?"

"The part where it's every man for himself!" Jerrika yelled before hurling a paperweight that was sitting on the desk at

Tommy.

She missed hitting Tommy, but it gave her enough of a distraction to run out of the office. She didn't get far before the sound of bullets erupted behind her. This was so not how Jerrika pictured she would die, in a rundown little colmado in a part of the Dominican Republic that tourists wouldn't dare step foot in.

"All this time, it was y'all!" Tommy roared as he let off shot after shot.

Jerrika ran, ducked, and hid behind large objects. The colmado was small, so she was running out of places to hide. She was now behind the industrial size freezer full of ice cream bars. Tommy shot it up until it had as many holes as a pair of old socks.

"Y'all was 'pose to be family!" Tommy hollered, rage coating every syllable he spat.

"Ahhhh!" Jerrika screamed as she ran out of the raining gunfire. Tommy stood right at the door, blocking her exit.

She was out of options. She was so afraid as tears sprinted down her face. She jumped over the counter and landed on her ass on the hard concrete flooring, scraping her elbows upon impact.

Gunz had always been the maniacal one of the twins, but that was now hard to tell by the way Tommy laughed like a lunatic. "You gon' die today, you treacherous bitch!"

He let off three more shots, causing the cash register to explode.

Jerrika scrambled for somewhere, anywhere to hide, but she'd made a terrible mistake jumping behind the counter. There was nowhere to go. She was now a sitting duck, waiting for the next bullet from Tommy's gun.

She knew this was her karma. She deserved to die, but that didn't mean she was ready for death or that she was going to just lie down and accept it. Her eyes darted desperately around until they landed on a silver handgun tucked beneath the counter. It sat in arm's reach in case the cashier needed to grab it quickly.

"Don't make me come back there and get yo' funky ass, Jerrika!" Tommy yelled, sending two more bullets behind the counter. One came so close to Jerrika that she heard and felt it whiz past her ear. She screamed and lunged toward Higuel's handgun.

Then she heard it... the sweetest sound she'd ever heard in her life, at the most perfect time... the click-click of Tommy's now empty gun.

She didn't wait for him to reload, or worse, pull out a second gun. She jumped up from behind the counter, holding Higuel's gun with both of her hands, and aimed it directly at Tommy.

"Fuck you!" She sneered at Tommy before unloading the gun into his body. She squeezed the trigger, until it was empty and Tommy lay motionless on the ground, leaking like a faucet.

The sound of sirens in the distance had her running out of the colmado as if it were on fire. She didn't check to see if Tommy was still breathing. She didn't look behind her. It was time for her to leave the Dominican Republic. She'd come too close to death tonight to stay in this country any longer. She jumped into her rental and sped off, tires screeching against the pavement, leaving only dust in her wake.

CHAPTER THIRTEEN

Duchess swiped at her tears before they fell into the donut batter. She wasn't supposed to be back at The Cookie Crumble. She was supposed to be on tour right now. She had no one to blame but herself. She'd thought with her heart and not with her mind when she hopped on that plane to the Dominican Republic. No second thoughts. No ifs or buts. Now she was suffering the repercussions of her hasty decision making.

She sniffed and continued to wipe away the tears. Just when things started to look like they were finally looking up, everything turned to shit. She was broke as hell and tossed the chance to live her dreams out of a window. On top of that, she was worried about her homegirl Jerrika. Nobody had heard from or seen her in days. Her heart was completely broken beyond repair, but that wasn't even the worst of it. The worst part of it all was having to live her life without Duke while he was alive, living life with another woman, and there was absolutely nothing she could do about any of it. Everything about life felt unfair to Duchess right now.

She gave herself a pity party for all of twenty minutes before sucking it up and putting on a happy face just in time to open the bakery.

She was in the back glazing the donuts when she heard the first customer enter the bakery. A few seconds later, Kimber called for Duchess.

She wiped her hands on her apron and walked out to the front. She wasn't sure who she expected to see, but it definitely wasn't her parents. Both of them stood behind the counter wearing opposite facial expressions. Her father wore a broad smile while her mother looked uneasy and as if she'd rather be sitting in the middle of hell.

Duchess couldn't remember the last time she'd seen her parents. She still harbored unforgiveness in her heart for her mother. They'd left things on a terrible note the last time they spoke, and Duchess hadn't reached out since.

"Duchess, baby!" Bennet said. "Come here, girl."

Duchess untied her apron and set it on the counter before walking out into her father's open arms. An hour earlier, she was on the verge of falling apart. In her father's arms, she did just that. She cried like a newborn baby, and it took Bennet completely by surprise. He looked at his wife, and she looked just as confused.

Pamela didn't know just what Duchess had been through since their falling out, but it really didn't matter. Seeing her baby girl fall apart in such a manner was all it took for her to forgive and forget every hurtful thing Duchess had said the day she kicked Pamela out of her home.

"Oh, Duchess, baby! What's wrong?" Pamela said before pulling her from Bennet and wrapping her arms around her.

"Everything," Duchess said. She hadn't planned on saying it, wasn't even sure why she was telling them. "Duke is alive."

"What!" Bennet and Pamela said at the same time.

"He's alive and living in the Dominican Republic with another woman."

Pamela sucked in her breath. She never liked Duke, but she would have never expected him to be this low down and dirty. She always thought he really loved Duchess.

"He doesn't know who he is though. He thinks he's someone else, and he won't come home to get help," Duchess continued. Once the well was open, she couldn't shut it. Before she knew it, she and her parents were seated, and she was telling them the whole story.

"Wow," Bennet said once Duchess had finished. While he was speechless, his mind was already in overdrive thinking of a solution for Duchess. He couldn't bear to see his daughter in this much pain and not try to fix it.

Pamela was terrified of saying the wrong thing. She and Duchess were finally mending their rocky relationship, so the last thing she wanted to do was say something to shove another wedge between them.

"Well, Duchess...maybe you should just let Duke go," she said slowly. "It sounds like he's started another life in the Dominican Republic, and he's happy. That's what's important, right? That's what you want, don't you? For Duke to be happy?"

Duchess thought about it. She wanted Duke to be happy more than anything in her life, even if that meant Duke without Duchess. Could she really do it, though? Could she let Duke go? It was one thing to let him go when she thought he was dead, but how would she do that knowing he was still on this Earth?

"Duchess?"

Everyone at the table looked up at Brian, who had entered the bakery and walked over to their table without them noticing.

"Brian!" Duchess wiped her face, not wanting Brian to know she was yet again crying over Duke.

"I wanted to stop by and say hello before I head into the office," he said, reaching to hug her. "Am I interrupting something?"

"Oh! No, not really. I was just talking to my parents." Duchess turned to look at them, and right away, she noticed Pamela sizing Brian up. "Momma and Daddy, this is Brian... my... uh...

friend."

Brian ignored the lackluster title Duchess had given him and shook both of her parents' hands. "It's nice to meet both of you."

"Nice handshake," Pamela said. She took in his fitted suit, clean shoes, and the fact he'd just said he was headed to the office. She almost immediately approved of him. "How long have you known my daughter, Brian?"

Brian looked at Duchess, and she shrugged. "A little over a year now, I believe."

"Ah," Pamela said. She saw how Brian looked at Duchess, and his body naturally leaned in to be closer to her. Just friends her ass! Pamela was far from a fool, and she could spot a man in love when she saw one. This Brian guy was definitely head over heels for Duchess.

"Brian, I was just about to invite Duchess over for dinner tonight. I'm cooking her favorite. How about you join her?"

"Momma, Brian can't. He's very bus—"

"I would love to," Brian said, interrupting Duchess. Maybe getting in good with her folks would make breaking down the wall surrounding Duchess's heart a little easier.

Duchess was seconds away from objecting, then she stopped herself. What the hell? She wasn't going to do anything but go home and cry herself to sleep. She needed a distraction, and tonight could possibly serve as the perfect one.

Pamela grinned so hard Duchess wondered how her face wasn't hurting. She'd never smiled at Duke in the way she was smiling at Brian. If Duchess didn't know better, she'd think her mother was even flirting with Brian.

Bennet was a bit more reserved, but it was obvious that he liked Brian as well. Like his wife, Bennet had never really cared much for Duke. His daughter deserved more than a street nigga. Unlike his wife, he never voiced that opinion to Duchess. He figured Duchess was a smart girl and would see that Duke wasn't the one, soon enough. That day never came though. If Duke hadn't died, Duchess would have married him. Bennet would never wish death on anyone, especially not someone his daughter loved so much, but at the same time, he was relieved she never made it down that aisle.

Now Brian, they could see as their son-in-law.

"So, tell me, Brian, what do you do for a living?" Bennet asked while fixing himself to a large helping of spicy lasagna.

"I'm the bank manager of Woods Bank," Brian said proudly. He'd worked his ass off to be promoted to manager of that bank, so he stuck his chest out whenever telling someone where he worked. He made a damn good living, but he knew Duchess was used to things he would need ten promotions to be able to afford.

"Woods Bank in North Dallas?" Bennet asked.

"Yes, sir."

"Ahh, yes. I know where that's at." Bennet winked at Duchess. "He's gainfully employed. I like this guy already."

Duchess rolled her eyes. She hoped that wasn't a dig at Duke.

"So how long have you and Duchess been dating?" Pamela asked.

"Oh no, Momma. We're not dating," Duchess corrected.

"Well, we were," Brian said, "until Duke came back from the dead."

"I imagine that could put a strain on things," Pamela said.

"Well, we don't have to worry about Duke anymore," Duchess said, desperately wanting to change the subject.

"Do we?" Brian asked.

Duchess was silent. This was not the time to have this conversation, especially with both of her parents in the room.

Brian continued. "Like I've told you a hundred times before, I'm willing to wait however long you need me to, but I need to know you want this. That I'm someone you can see yourself with."

Duchess swallowed hard. Her mouth was dry as sandpaper all of a sudden. She reached for her glass of water and gulped it down. All eyes were on her, and she grew hot under the intensity of the moment.

"Duchess?" Brian asked.

"Yes, I can see myself with you, Brian," she said. She felt like she was under pressure and wished Brian could see that in her rigid body language and stop this conversation.

Unfortunately, Duchess didn't realize it, but she had just given Brian the greenlight with her response. Hearing that she still wanted him was all he needed to know. He reached into his coat and pulled out a black velvet box.

Pamela screeched with excitement.

Bennet hooted.

Duchess hoped that wasn't what she thought it was.

Brian knelt on one knee and took Duchess's left hand. "Duchess, since the moment I met you, I knew there was something special about you. You were broken, and I was committed to putting all the broken pieces of you back together. I know you have been through hell and back, but I want you to know that you don't have to go through any of that alone anymore... not as

THE DUKE AND DUCHESS OF DALLAS 2

long as you have me. I want you to be my wife, Duchess."

"Brian…" She was speechless, but she also knew this wasn't what she wanted. It hadn't even been a full month since she found out Duke was still alive. How in the world did Brian expect her to even consider marrying him?

"I'm not saying we have to do it next month. We don't even have to do it next year, but I want you to be my wife, Duchess. So what do you say?"

Duchess nervously chewed on her bottom lip. The last thing she wanted to do was say no to Brian in front of her parents, but she couldn't say yes to him. She couldn't marry him. Her heart was still in the Dominican Republic, so how could she give it to Brian?

Then, she heard Demarcus's voice and felt the searing pain of his hurtful words as he told her he felt nothing for her, as he told her he wasn't Duke and never would be. He'd started a new life and all but erased Duke's existence, so why should Duchess put her life on hold? Why should she look at this beautiful man kneeling in front of her, promising her the world, and say no?

Maybe this was meant to be. Maybe there was never meant to be a forever for Duke and Duchess. Maybe it was time for her to let Duke go for good.

"Yes," she said to Brian's and her own amazement. "Yes, Brian. I'll marry you."

Pamela and Bennet clapped and cheered. Duchess had no idea Brian had already asked them both for Duchess's hand in marriage hours earlier. They hadn't known Brian long, but they were completely smitten with him.

Brian slid the ring on Duchess's finger and then picked her up and spun her around. "I'm gonna make you the happiest woman in the world, Duchess. I give you my word on that," Brian promised.

Duchess believed him.

CHAPTER FOURTEEN

The Policía Nacional Dominicana ruled Tommy's death as a robbery gone wrong since both he and the shop's owner were found dead, but Ford and Gunz didn't believe that shit. They knew for a fact Tommy had gone to the store to pick up cigarillos and not to rob the place.

Ford thought he'd seen every side of Gunz there was to see. The rage bathing inside of him was something Ford had never seen, and it kind of scared him. Gunz had always been a blood thirsty loose cannon, and now he ran around the Dominican Republic as a ticking timebomb, ready to explode at any moment.

Ford and Gunz were tore up over Tommy's death. It was like reliving Duke's death all over again, only this time they knew it was real. Ford had never been good with words, so he didn't know what to say to comfort Gunz. He couldn't say it would be alright because it wouldn't ever be alright again. Tommy was his twin. They'd shared everything since the womb. Ford didn't know that level of loss.

"I gotta find out who killed my brother, Ford," Gunz said.

"We will."

"I need to find out who did that shit, ASAP." Gunz's eyes were bloodshot, and his voice was hoarse. Ford didn't think he'd seen Gunz sleep at all in the days since finding out about Tommy's death.

"You still think Rico ain't have shit to do with what happened to Duke?" Gunz asked. "Niggas came after us and then my brother ends up dead. Shai ain't did that, Ford. So you tell me, do you still trust that nigga Rico?"

Ford didn't know what to say. He fully believed Shai was responsible for what happened to his brother, but he had to admit, all of this was a little too coincidental to overlook. Getting at Rico a second time wouldn't be easy. It'd damn near be impossible.

"I don't trust Rico. I never said I trusted him, but I really don't think this has his name on it."

Gunz looked like he was seconds away from exploding. He jumped to his feet. "Then who did the shit, Ford? Who in this country would want to fuck with us? Who wants us dead?"

Ford was afraid to voice who he really thought. He didn't want to put a bull's-eye on his back like that. He fully believed Demarcus was behind all of this.

Ever since she'd come home from the hospital, Demarcus had been treating Auri like a piece of glass, and she loved every second of it. He hadn't forgotten what she'd done, but he hadn't mentioned it. In fact, he was being more loving and attentive than ever. Auri didn't think it was possible to fall any deeper in love with Demarcus, but each day, she fell harder.

"You need anything, babe?" Demarcus asked, poking his head into the bedroom where Auri lay down.

"No. You heading out?"

"Yeah. I gotta make a run real quick. I'll be back in a couple of hours."

"OK. I love you."

"I love you too."

Auri almost died. She'd been stupid as hell and almost lost her life because of it. Her near death experience saved her marriage, so she didn't regret it at all. She hadn't heard from Jerrika since that night, and she wondered if she'd pop back up at her doorstep with another murderous plan. Auri would turn her away this time though. She was the wife of a boss and would never pick up another gun. She didn't need to. Demarcus was going to handle Ford for her. She'd planted the seed in his head, and now it was only a matter of time before Ford was out of their lives completely.

She no longer even had to worry about Duchess. Demarcus told her he'd sent Duchess back to the States after telling her he didn't want anything to do with her. Things couldn't have worked out better for Auri. Demarcus knew the truth, and he stayed. He now knew everything, but he still chose Auri. Life was fantastic!

Demarcus left the port after checking on their latest shipment. Everything went smoothly, so he was in a good mood. He decided to stop by one of Auri's favorite spots to grab some takeout. It was dark as hell, and he was on his cell, not paying attention to his surroundings as he walked toward his car.

He felt cold steel against the back of his head and stopped in his tracks. He ended the call and slid his phone into his pocket. He lifted both of his hands in the air. "Look, I haven't seen ya face, so you're good. I'm gonna give you a five-minute head start to get the fuck outta here before you make the biggest mistake of your life."

"Why did you kill Tommy?" Ford asked.

Demarcus immediately recognized Ford's voice. He sighed and shook his head. This little nigga just wouldn't quit! How many death wishes did he have?

"I don't know what the fuck you talking about," Demarcus said.

"He was like a brother to me! You ain't had to do him like that! What the fuck did he ever do to you?"

"I said, I don't know what you talking about!"

"Shut the fuck up!" Ford had started crying, and he hated it. He'd loved Tommy, and he loved his brother, but this nigga wasn't his brother. He wasn't Duke. He was Demarcus, and he had to pay for what he'd done.

"I don't know, Duke. I don't know what happened. I know we did a lot of shit—a lot of dirt and committed a lot of sins. But I don't think we deserved this shit. You losing your memory and shit, going against the grain, coming after me and then Tommy —shit ain't right, man."

Ford's hand was unsteady, and emotions had him all over the place. He didn't want to kill his brother, but he didn't have a choice. Duke was already gone. This nigga was just wearing his skin. He felt like he was dying inside. He'd lost Tommy, and now he was about to lose Duke for good.

"You talkin' about one of them twins?" Demarcus asked.

"You know who I'm fucking talking about!"

"Ford, listen. If I bodied a nigga, I'd admit it. I don't have no reason to lie to you. I didn't hurt your friend. My beef ain't with him. It's with you."

Ford wasn't sure if he just wanted to believe Demarcus so bad or if it was the authenticity in his voice, but he believed him. He lowered his gun.

Demarcus spun around and punched Ford in the face. The blow had Ford stunned, but he quickly recovered and threw several punches of his own. He hadn't fought his older brother since they were kids—never had a reason to. Tonight, they weren't brothers. They fought like two niggas on the street that had real beef.

"I didn't kill ya friend, but I'ma kill you!" Demarcus hollered.

"I didn't touch your fuckin' lyin' ass wife! That bitch is lying, just like she lied about everything else!"

Demarcus and Ford rolled around on the ground, tussling, both of them winded.

Neither one of them had much fight left in them and eventually separated, both breathing heavy, knuckles bruised and bleeding.

"I'mma tell you like I told Duchess," Demarcus said while trying to catch his breath, "go back home. You looking for Duke, but Duke is dead, and he ain't coming back. There ain't nothing here for you anymore."

Ford was starting to believe it. He wasn't sure how much longer he could stay in this country waiting on Duke's memories to return, especially when Demarcus wasn't trying to let that happen. Plus, he had to get back to Dallas and handle Shai's ass. Not to mention, someone was out to get him and Gunz. Ford had never run from a nigga in his life, and he wasn't about to start now, but maybe it was time to throw in the towel.

"I know you loved your brother, and I don't even wanna know how it felt to lose him. But he ain't coming back, Ford. Go back home and try to move on with your life."

It was easy for Demarcus to say that. He wasn't the one with the hole in his soul, but he was right. Ford was finally ready to admit it.

It was time for him to go back home.

Auri and Levi were asleep by the time Demarcus made it home. He took a shower and climbed into bed with his wife and son. This was his life. It wasn't perfect; his wife had her faults, but she was his, and he wasn't going to turn his back on her. He kissed the back of her neck before huddling closer to the warmth of her body. He thought about Duchess and Ford before falling asleep. He wished them luck and only hoped they had the strength to forget about him.

SIX MONTHS LATER...

Chapter Fifteen

"What time this nigga getting here, Shai?" Duke looked at his Rolex for the third time in the last ten minutes. He grew impatient. This wasn't how he did business. Rico Ree was supposed to pull up next to them in the middle of the sea on some next level, drug dealing shit, but he and Shai had been here for at least forty-five minutes, and there wasn't another boat in sight.

"I don't know," Shai said. "He said he'd meet us at noon." Shai's nerves were getting the best of him. He wasn't sure he could really go through with this, but at the same time, he would never be able to face Jerrika if he came back home talking about he'd punked out of the plan.

Duke had to die.

"I don't like this shit, Shai. I got a real bad feeling," Duke said *before sitting down. His instinct told him something wasn't right about this situation.*

He should have never let Shai talk him into not bringing Ford and the twins. If it came down to gunplay with Rico and his goons, Shai wouldn't be much help. He'd never been that thorough. These days, Duke wondered why he even kept him on the payroll. Yeah, he was his boy, but he was becoming more of a liability than an asset.

Duke checked the time on his watch again. He jumped up from his seat. "Man, fuck this." He headed toward the boat's captain. "Turn this muthafucka around. We going back."

The captain nodded but looked at Shai for confirmation. Shai was the one who was paying him. He knew beforehand what was about to go down, so turning back around wasn't an option.

"Chill out, Duke," Shai said. His palms were sweaty as hell. He was a nervous wreck. How the hell would he be able to successfully go through with this shit? "Here, drink some of this to relax your damn nerves."

Duke took the drink from Shai and gulped it down. The Hennessy went down so smooth, Duke never tasted the sedative crushed into the drink. Twenty minutes later, he felt it. He was so drowsy, he could barely keep his eyes open. That on top of the way that the boat bounced on top of the waves, had Duke almost on his ass.

He was so out of it that he laughed when Shai pulled a gun on him. He thought it was a joke. He was half-sleep and thought he was dreaming.

"I'm sorry, Duke. I didn't want it to come to this," Shai said, his voice as wobbly as the boat. "You left me no choice. You starving me out here, man."

"Huh? What the fuck you talkin' about, Shai?" Duke struggled to focus. Everything was going blurry, his head was spinning, and he felt nauseous as if he were about to get seasick.

Shai shook his head. He didn't owe Duke an explanation. He had to get this over with. He cocked the gun and tried to steady his trembling hand.

The sound of the hammer being pulled back told Duke he wasn't dreaming. He knew that sound anywhere. He lunged toward Shai. Under any other circumstances, he could have taken Shai with one hand tied behind his back, but being drugged handicapped Duke and made him an easy target.

Shai left off two shots that put Duke on his back. Duke's eyes were wide with shock, and both of his hands were on his chest, trying to stop the blood seeping out of him.

"Help me with him!" Shai called out to the captain.

Together, they lifted Duke from the boat and tossed him overboard.

"You sure he's dead?" the captain asked.

Shai was sure, but for good measure, he sent several more shots into the ocean in the same spot they'd just dumped Duke.

Duke felt himself sinking. He felt the water over his head, in his ears, and in his nostrils. He was drowning.

Panic hit him as he realized he was dying and he'd never see Duchess again.

"Duchess..." he whispered before everything went black.

Duke shot upright in bed. His chest heaved rapidly at the dream he had, only it wasn't a dream. It was a memory! His nigga had tried to kill him! Both of Duke's hands went to his chest in search of bullet holes. While his fingers traced his bare chest, he noticed his unfamiliar surroundings.

"What the fuck?"

He was in a bed that didn't belong to him, in a room that wasn't his. He jumped out of the bed and searched the night-stand for his cell phone. He had to call Duchess and tell her what

Shai had done! He had to get word to Ford immediately!

"Muthafucka!" Duke howled as he punched his fist inside his open palm. He was so angry, he had the urge to punch the wall, but he couldn't do anything until he figured out where the fuck he was.

"What's wrong? Why you in here screaming?" Auri asked as she walked into their bedroom. The look on Demarcus's face froze her in place. "What's wrong?"

Duke's face curled in confusion and then anger. "Who the fuck are you?"

"What?" Auri didn't know what else to say.

Duke ran his hand over his head. "Look, I don't know what the fuck is going on right now, but I need to find my phone."

"Demarcus?"

Duke turned around and took a longer look at Auri. Her face was familiar, but he couldn't put his finger on it. Then, it hit him! This was the chick from the strip club from last night! He shook his head. He knew he hadn't... he couldn't have!

"Demarcus, you're scaring me," Auri said, her voice laced with fear.

"Who the fuck is Demarcus?"

Auri gasped. No, no, no! This couldn't be happening. "Duke?"

"Look, shorty, I need to find my phone. I don't know what happened between us last night, but it was a mistake. I'm engaged. I'm about to get married."

Auri fell to her knees. How was this happening? Last night, they'd made love in hopes of making another child. He'd fallen asleep in their bed as Demarcus. This morning, he'd awoken as Duke. No warning signs, no symptoms, not even a memory. Just wham, he was Duke again. And worst of all, he didn't have a clue who she was.

Duke frantically searched through the comforter and sheets for his cell phone. He didn't know why shorty was tripping, crying and acting a fool. He didn't have time to worry about it. All he could think about was Shai... Shai's double crossing, snake in the grass, jealous-hearted ass!

Auri was losing her mind. She didn't know what to say or do. Obviously, Demarcus was no more, and Duke had come to reclaim his mind. She hadn't been prepared for this because she had no idea this could even happen.

The sound of Levi wailing stopped Auri's own tears. Somehow in her moment of distress, she'd forgotten all about their son. She got up from the floor and ran toward him. Surely once Duke laid eyes on Levi, he would remember his son, right? There was no way he could ever forget that kind of love or bond.

She raced to Levi, picked him up, and ran back into their master bedroom. "Demarcus! Please, look!"

Duke didn't know why this chick kept calling him Demarcus. Something was obviously wrong with her. Something was wrong with him too. What the fuck was he thinking going home with this chick? How did that happen? When did that happen? The last thing he remembered was Shai and the boat's captain tossing him overboard the yacht. He remembered being shot and being so drowsy that he could barely control his own limbs. He remembered drowning. He remembered his last words being a whisper of Duchess's name.

So how in the hell did he wake up in this woman's bed?

Auri ran up to Duke and shoved Levi into his arms. "Look! Take him! He's your son. Don't you remember?"

Duke took several steps back. Oh, this bitch was crazy, crazy!

Levi stopped crying as soon as he was in his daddy's arms.

He cooed at Duke, but Duke gawked back at the young child in puzzlement.

He didn't recognize Levi. Auri's shoulders slumped. This was it. This was the end of everything. Her fairy tale life was gone.

She retrieved Duke's cell phone from the chest of drawers. She searched through the contact list until she found the number she was looking for. "Here. Call Rico. He will explain everything to you." She took Levi from Duke's arms then turned and walked out of the bedroom while closing the door behind her.

Rico? Duke's head felt like it was seconds away from exploding. He had a throbbing headache, and on top of that, nothing made sense. He stared at the unfamiliar cell phone in his hands. He wasn't about to call Rico! He had to reach out to his brother before Shai had the chance to get at him.

Duke scrolled through the phone, unfamiliar with how it worked. His eyes widened; he blinked several times because he was sure his mind was playing tricks on him. The date at the top of the screen had to be wrong. Something was fucked-up about this phone because the date was reading two years in the future. Duke's bachelor party was only two days ago, but the date on this phone said it'd been over two years ago!

Duke sat on top of the bed, suddenly feeling lightheaded. He continued scrolling through the phone until he came across the gallery. He clicked into it and saw several photos of himself with the same little boy ol' girl shoved at him!

What the fuck?

Photos on top of photos that Duke didn't remember taking were in his face, and then there were photos of him and the chick! Photos of them kissing... photos of his hand on her pregnant belly... photos of them dressed in white on a beach, getting married!

The phone slipped from Duke's hand.

CHAPTER SIXTEEN

Ford looked both ways before crossing the street. He didn't think anyone was following him, but he had to make sure. He had his hoodie low so his eyes couldn't be seen. He couldn't afford anyone in this hood recognizing him.

He hopped into the white Caprice Classic waiting for him. "How many niggas in there?" Gunz asked before putting the car in drive and peeling off the block.

"About six," Ford said with a smile. "Their whole operation sloppy."

Gunz grinned as he and Ford bumped fists. They'd been back in Dallas for six months, robbing Shai's traps. The streets had no idea they'd returned to the city, so no one even suspected them. Ford planned on killing Shai, but first he wanted to hit him where it hurt the most—that nigga's pockets. It was the least he could do. Money was Shai's motive for betraying Duke, so money was what Ford would take before he took his life.

They'd kept a low profile while also keeping their ears to the streets. Shai had GMB on lock, but the clique didn't respect him like Duke. Their loyalty was waning, and Ford planned on taking full advantage of that weakness. He no longer had any love for GMB. When it came time to avenge his brother's death, not one single member stepped up. So, to him, it was fuck GMB.

Ford still kept in touch with Duchess. They vowed to never lose touch again. He hated that she was marrying that corny ass nigga, Brian, but he couldn't blame her. It was time for her to move on; Duke was dead.

When they made it onto 635 Highway and got jammed up in traffic, Gunz slowed the car to a creep. "So how many more spots of Shai's we gonna hit before we hit that nigga?"

In the beginning, it'd been fun robbing Shai, but now Gunz was bored. His hunger for blood and revenge was escalating and needed to be fed. After getting rid of Shai and taking over GMB, they were going to head right back to the DR with the army they needed to get at Rico. That's what Ford had promised Gunz, and everyday Gunz grew more and more impatient. They'd returned to Dallas broke, but after hitting up so many of Shai's spots, they now had more than enough money. Gunz didn't care about the money, especially since his brother wasn't here to share it with.

"This the last one," Ford said.

Gunz looked at his best friend. He hadn't expected that answer as a wide grin spread across his face.

"We do this one tonight, and tomorrow we pay Shai a visit," Ford continued. He was ready. He'd been laying low, learning the way Shai moved for six months. It was time to put that nigga in the ground where he tried to put his brother.

"That's what I'm talkin' 'bout!" Gunz hollered. Shai was the reason everything had gone wrong. If it wasn't for his disloyalty, Duke wouldn't have ever lost his memory, and Tommy wouldn't have lost his life. Yeah, Gunz was ready to kill Shai's bitch ass.

The car moved down the highway slowly in the bumper-to-bumper traffic, making Ford and Gunz restless. Ford's phone began vibrating in his pocket. He pulled it out and was shocked into immobility seeing Demarcus's name on his screen. He hadn't talked to him since he left the Dominican Republic. Even then, it'd been on bad terms. He didn't expect to hear from that nigga ever again.

"Yo," Ford answered, not sure what to expect.

"Ford!" Demarcus's voice sounded strained and relieved at the same time. Something about the way he shouted Ford's name made him sit up straight in the car.

"Yeah?"

"Ford, what the fuck is going on, man? Where you at? Shit don't make any sense... I need you to come get me, bro. I don't know... I don't understand... I feel like I'm going crazy, bro!"

Ford instantly knew. Even though his sentences were choppy, erratic, and disordered, Ford knew.

Duke was back.

CHAPTER SEVENTEEN

Duchess felt a stab of déjà vu as she listened to her wedding planner speak. Two years ago, she and Ingrid sat in this very office discussing the details of her upcoming nuptials to the love of her life.

Today, she did the very same thing, except now, the groom was Brian. She didn't love him with the very depth of her soul as she'd loved Duke, but over time, she learned to love Brian. He'd been by her side every single day. He'd become a permanent fixture in her life. He was supportive, loving, compassionate to her need to take things slow, and gentle with her heart. How could she not love that man?

Duchess's mother sat next to her, smiling like a Cheshire cat, the complete opposite of how she'd been when they sat in this same office, planning her wedding when she was marrying Duke. Duchess couldn't help but shake her head and feel some type of way. Why couldn't Pamela have been this supportive then? Duchess had been excited beyond words then. Now, she felt as if she were just going through the motions.

When Brian proposed, he said they could wait as long as she needed. Yet, here they were, six months later, planning the wedding of the century. Duchess wanted to wait, but her mother pummeled her with questions as to what the point was in waiting. Duchess wasn't getting any younger. She loved Brian, and he loved her, so really, what was the point?

Duchess had to agree. She dared not tell her mother that her heart was still in the Dominican Republic, and every day she woke up praying this was the day it'd return to her. Pamela would and could never understand. Besides, Duchess had put her own interest aside far too many times when it came to Duke. She'd never returned to college once they started dating. She'd put her dreams of becoming a professional singer to the side, not once but twice for Duke! And what had she gotten in return? Nothing.

Brian told her once they were married, he wanted her to quit working at the bakery. He promised to take care of her financially, but Duchess refused. Never again would she be financially dependent on a man. She'd already started taking classes at Eastfield College and had plans to finally get that degree she'd abandoned years ago. She hadn't given up on her singing aspirations either. She started taking vocal lessons on the weekends and had her first showcase in a month at a lounge downtown.

She wasn't where she wanted to be, but she was on her way.

"What do you think about that table placement, Duchess? I was thinking about placing your uncle Leroy across the room from your aunt Elle because they're going through that nasty divorce right now," Pamela said.

Duchess blinked her eyes several times. She hadn't heard a word Ingrid and Pamela had been discussing. "Uh, sure. Yeah, sounds great."

Two hours later, Duchess dropped her mother off at home and was meeting Billie for lunch. Everything had gone great today, but for some reason, she felt off.

Billie noticed it as soon as Duchess sat down across from her. "Miss Pam give you hell today?"

"Naw. She's actually been on her best behavior. I can't remember the last time I saw my momma this excited about anything," Duchess said.

"Well, what's up with that look on your face?"

Duchess shrugged. "I don't know, Billie. I know I'm supposed to be happy, but I'm not."

Billie frowned and set her fork down. "You think you moving too fast with the wedding stuff?"

"Kinda. I mean, I know any woman would kill to be in my shoes. Brian is the epitome of a good man. He's everything and more, and I do love him. I really do... It's just..."

"You still love Duke," Billie said.

Duchess nodded, feeling stupid. "I can't explain it. It's just hard for me to move on with my life knowing he's still alive, and he's stuck over there in that country living another life. As crazy as this sounds, I think I probably could deal with it better if he really was dead."

"That's how you have to look at it, Duchess. If you're ever going to be able to move on with your life, you have to see Duke as dead."

"I can't do that, Billie."

Billie sighed; this was a losing battle, a dead-end conversation. "I don't know what to tell you, Duchess. I know you love Duke, that you probably always will, but Duke is in the Dominican Republic married to another woman. You have to accept that and move on. Don't risk losing a man that loves you, chasing after the ghost of a man that no longer remembers you."

Billie's words stung, and it was all over Duchess's face. Billie didn't want to hurt her girl; she just needed her to see what was at stake here. She'd never forgive herself for not stopping Duchess from hopping on that plane to the Dominican Republic, when she should have been on a plane headed to tour with Leela Lennox. Billie wouldn't let her girl make another mistake that severe again.

"Anyway," Duchess said, wanting to change the subject before she got in her feelings. "Have you heard from Jerrika?"

Duchess had tried calling Jerrika for weeks once she got back to Dallas, but Jerrika had changed her number. She also moved into a new home that Billie and Duchess didn't have the address to. At first, Duchess was worried about her girl, but judging by the photos she posted on social media, Jerrika was doing just fine.

"No! That bitch blocked me on social media," Billie said. "I tried sending her a couple of DMs to see why she ghosted me like that on the DR trip, and she blocked me! I don't know, Duchess. Something doesn't feel right about that."

Duchess nodded, but she didn't want to let her mind go there. It was almost unthinkable. If she were to believe Ford, Shai had something to do with what happened to Duke. It wasn't that farfetched to suspect Jerrika may have had a hand in it as well. Duchess would have never suspected her girl had Jerrika not started moving funny.

"I don't wanna say it, but maybe..." Billie couldn't even finish her thought. Jerrika was a lot of things, but she wasn't a murderer. Besides, she'd been by Duchess the entire time she mourned Duke. She couldn't have done that if she'd been involved, right? There was no way Jerrika was that cold blooded. They'd all once been really close. They knew Jerrika, and that didn't seem like her at all. Then again, it also didn't seem like Shai, but now they all knew the truth.

"Every day I turn on the news, I expect to see Shai's death being reported," Duchess admitted. "Ford and Gunz aren't gonna let something like that slide."

Billie nodded. "Girl, I know." She was about to elaborate on the subject when she noticed Brian entering the restaurant and heading in their direction. "Uh oh, looks like we have a guest joining us."

Duchess turned around only to be greeted by Brian's smiling face. He bent to kiss her. "Don't get up." He slid into the booth and smiled at Billie. "How you doing, Billie?"

"I'm good."

"I hope I'm not interrupting no girl talk," he said.

"You kinda are," Duchess said, annoyed by his sudden appearance. "What are you doing here?"

"Your mother told me you were here having lunch. I got off early today and wanted to see my fiancée." He smiled, oblivious to the irritation on Duchess's face and shift in her body language.

He waved over the waiter and asked for a menu. "How did the meeting with the planner go today?"

"Fine," Duchess said.

Billie liked Brian and all, but sometimes he seemed so overbearing. He was obviously head over heels in love with Duchess, but sometimes, his love looked like obsession. Billie knew Brian was a good guy and good for Duchess, but if he didn't chill out, he was going to push her away.

"That's good," Brian said. "Did she say how much this wedding is gonna cost me?" He chuckled. He really didn't care how much the wedding cost because he was marrying the woman of his dreams. There was no way to put a price tag on something so priceless. He smiled at Duchess, unable to believe his luck, unable to believe he was really going to get the chance to call this woman his wife.

"You look amazing today, babe," Brian said, kissing Duchess again.

"Thanks," she said, blushing under the intensity of his stare.

"I was talking to my moms the other day, and she came up

with a good idea," Brian said. "How about for our honeymoon, we tour the coast of France?"

"Sounds amazing but expensive as hell," Duchess said.

"You let me worry about that," he said with confidence. He couldn't compare with her ex financially, but he'd go into debt to put a smile on Duchess's face.

Duchess couldn't help but notice the way Brian smiled at her. Like she was the center of his universe and the reason he got up every morning. Billie's words replayed in her head.

"Don't risk losing a man that loves you, chasing after the ghost of a man that no longer remembers you."

It was obvious Brian loved her. She was lucky to experience the real love of not one but two men. One was gone forever, but the other sat right next to her, smiling at her, unable to keep his hands off her, and unable to stop staring lovingly at her. She wasn't blind, and she wasn't a fool. It was time for her to stop taking Brian for granted. It was time for her to be happy she was becoming his wife.

CHAPTER EIGHTEEN

Duke stood in the US Customs line at DFW International Airport. He clutched his passport with sweaty palms. The meeting he'd had with Rico Ree yesterday still had his head spinning. Everything he'd learned sounded like something out of a science fiction movie and was still hard to believe.

Auri had called Rico over to the house out of fear that Duke was going to attack her. Truthfully, he was on the verge of doing just that. Nothing made sense, and she was all in his face calling him Demarcus and shit.

Rico had been expecting this ever since the day Dr. Peña told him it was a possibility Duke would regain his memory and lose the others. He showed up at the house with a box Ford had left with him. It contained Duke's passport, Texas driver's license, and a lot of other items that only Duke would recognize. Rico had done his best to explain to Duke what the last two years of his life had been, but Duke was so aggressive and distrustful that nothing Rico said seemed to get through to him. He'd done his best, purchased a one-way ticket to Dallas for Duke, and left the house knowing he'd never see his second-in-command, Demarcus Jones, again.

Duke made his way through the long line and checkpoint. It seemed like forever before he finally exited the airport.

Ford and Gunz were parked in the arrival lane, eyes glued to the exit. When they finally spotted Duke, they both jumped out of the car and ran toward him like Duke was an inmate finally being released from prison.

Finally seeing familiar faces meant the world to Duke. His head was a mess, but seeing his brother silenced the craziness for a second.

"Duke? Is it really you, my nigga?" Ford asked after hugging him.

Duke grinned. "Who else, nigga?"

"Shit, Demarcus. That's who," Gunz cracked. "You was down in the Dominican straight tripping, fool, walking around talking about yo' name was Demarcus and shit."

Ford and Gunz laughed, but Duke's face went stoic. To him, this shit wasn't a joke. He'd lost two years of his life that he could never get back.

They walked to the Caprice, and Duke got in the front seat while Ford hopped behind the wheel.

"Take me to Duchess," Duke said as soon as Ford started the car. He'd opted not to call Duchess since regaining his memory. Some conversations had to be in person, and this was one of them.

"Uh, I don't know about that, fam," Ford said.

Duke's head snapped in Ford's direction. "What the hell you talkin' about?"

"A lot has changed since you been gone, Duke. I mean, we thought you was dead. We thought Rico had bodied you. We had a funeral and everything. Shit went to shit round here. Duchess lost the house... had to get a job. She even had to—"

"What you mean she lost the house!" Duke yelled. Both of his fists were balled. It was bad enough he felt like a science fair project, but he was learning that his brother hadn't looked out for his woman while he was gone.

"Like I said," Ford continued, "she lost the house. She lost everything! She trusted Shai and gave him all the stuff you kept at the house. She didn't tell me shit until it was too late!"

"Muthafucka!" Duke slammed his fist into his open palm. He saw red, and his blood boiled. He was going to that dark place of no return.

"At the time, we still trusted Shai. We didn't know what the nigga did," Ford said. "We was thinkin' Rico was the trigger man. Me, Tommy, and Gunz packed up and moved to the DR. Shit wasn't the same in Dallas anyway. Niggas was coming for my head. Respect was dead."

Duke had to take several deep breaths to calm himself so he could listen to his brother. He needed to hear this; he needed to know everything that took place while he was gone.

"We knew the odds was against us, but we came to the DR anyway and infiltrated Rico's crew. It took a whole fuckin' year, but I was able to finally get in the same room as the man. Right when I had my gun to his head, bam! Here you come knocking me the fuck out."

Gunz laughed in the back seat of the car, and Ford joined him.

"Shit was wild, Duke. I mean, all this time we thought you was dead. Here I am on some Rambo shit, trying to kill the man I thought had killed you, and there you were with a gun pointed in my face."

"Damn," Duke said, shaking his head. How could that have happened? How could he have pulled a gun on Ford?

"I knew something was wrong with you because your eyes were dead. You was staring at me like you'd never seen me before. I tried explaining who I was, but you shot me... twice."

Duke didn't think anything could shock him more than he already was. Ford's words proved him wrong. "I shot you?" Emotions had Duke's voice wobbling.

Ford nodded. "It wun shit, though. I was wearing a vest."

"I shot you," Duke repeated as if that made it easier to believe.

"I knew then you wasn't Duke," Ford said. "The nigga Rico stopped you before you could empty your clip in my head. And once you was gone, we chopped it up. He knew I wasn't lying when I said you was my brother. He tried to help me. He tried to help all of us, but you wasn't hearing any of the shit, Duke. Duchess dropped everything once I called and flew to the DR."

Duke's heart did a couple of somersaults in his chest. He shut his eyes, wishing he could turn back the clock and go back to that very moment. How he was able to lay eyes on Duchess and not remember her seemed asinine.

"I broke her heart?" Duke asked, already knowing the answer. Duchess believed he was dead for over a year, only to find him living with another woman and kid in the Dominican Republic, with no memory of her. He winced as he thought about what that had to do to Duchess.

"Yeah," Ford said solemnly.

"Take me to her now, Ford," Duke demanded. He'd heard enough. He had to fix this shit right now.

"She's moved on, yo. She's finally happy again. She wit' another nigga." Ford didn't want to say it. He'd thought for days how he'd break it to Duke.

"What!" Duke felt as if he would explode in the car. He felt as if his head would combust right then and there.

"She getting married, bro."

Duke shook his head. "Naw, naw, naw."

"Think about it. You got married and had a kid... told her to go back to Dallas and move on with her life 'cause Duke was dead and never comin' back. So that's what she did. She didn't have a choice, Duke." Ford tried to reason with his brother.

Duke knew he was being irrational expecting Duchess to still be single two years later, expecting her to be waiting with bated breath for a man that may or may not have ever returned to her, but still, that's what he expected. So what he'd married someone else and had a child with her. He couldn't see Duchess with anyone other than him. Tears of hurt, anger, and unreasonable wrath welled in his eyes.

"I'm going to kill Shai," he said. His voice was emotionless, even toned, and a matter of a fact.

"Let's not forget about Rico," Gunz said from the back seat. "He killed my brother."

"What?" Duke looked to Ford for explanation.

Ford's eyes darted nervously. Tommy's death was still a mystery to him. He couldn't find motive for Rico wanting Tommy dead. He'd pacified Gunz ever since they touched down in Dallas because he believed he'd have answers before it came down to actually going to war with Rico.

Gunz went on a rant explaining why he thought Rico had been the triggerman. Duke was silent as he spoke, but once Gunz finished, Duke knew Rico hadn't been involved. He didn't know or trust Rico, but Gunz's story didn't add up.

"Someone else killed Tommy," he said flatly.

"What the fuck? How you figure?" Gunz sat up straight. Duke had gotten his memory back a couple of days ago, so how the fuck did he know?

Duke hadn't been crowned the Duke of Dallas for no reason. He was intelligent, witty, and easily peeped game. How Shai escaped Duke was beyond him. There were so many signs he'd ignored out of loyalty to a snake.

Even so, he was as sharp as they came. "I just know. Trust me on this, G."

Gunz couldn't swallow that. His mouth opened, and a rebuttal was on the tip of his tongue.

"I promise, we won't rest until Tommy's killer is laying in the ground alongside Shai," Duke said.

Duke's word was gold and enough for Gunz. He sat back, knowing whoever killed his brother wouldn't live to see the New Year.

Duke returned his attention to Ford. "I hear everything you saying about Duchess, but I need to see her, fam. That's my wife, man. I can't be in the same city and not see her. I know it's been two years, but to me, it's not even been a week. I woke up this morning thinking my bachelor party had just been two days ago! I can't just sit on the sidelines and let Duchess marry some nigga without at least seeing her and pleading my case."

Ford sighed. This was a losing argument. All he could do was hope Duchess's fiancé wasn't around when they popped up.

CHAPTER NINETEEN

Jerrika shook her head in disgust as she watched Shai rant and rave about how he was about to set the city on fire behind his spots being robbed one after the other. He was all talk; he didn't have it in him to body anyone. Hell, he couldn't even properly kill Duke's ass.

Ever since Jerrika found out Duke was alive, she'd begun to lose respect for Shai. The respect was the first thing to go, then the love. She now stared at him wondering what she ever saw in his ass. He wasn't fit to be the King of Dallas. Niggas tried him left and right, and he didn't do shit about it. He was being clowned in the streets, and it wouldn't be long before he lost their respect as well. Then it was all over for Shai, and it'd be open season on his life.

Jerrika didn't plan to be around long enough to see that happen. She had to find a replacement for Shai as fast as possible, if she wanted to remain on the throne. She'd be damned if she let Shai take her down with him.

She still hadn't told him what she'd found out about Duke. What was the point? Shai wasn't worth a damn and couldn't do anything about it. Hell, she barely could fix the situation. She'd went to the DR and sought out Ford unsuccessfully, nearly getting herself killed in the process. Ford was still a threat to their organization if he helped Duke get his memory back, but Jerrika couldn't worry herself about that... not now at least. She had to secure the throne, or there wouldn't be a kingdom to defend if Duke ever did come back.

"So what you gonna do about it!" she snapped. "All I hear is a lot of bitching and whining."

Shai stopped mid-rant and glared at Jerrika. Here he was, losing crazy money, and instead of helping him fix the shit, she came at him. He side-eyed her, wondering if she had a hand in this sudden string of robberies. He couldn't put anything past Jerrika.

"I'm saying," she continued while filing her nails, "you talkin' big shit right now, but you haven't done a thing to stop the hits. In fact, just two nights ago, they touched the West Dallas spot, the one you was just so sure was untouchable."

"Niggas is trying me, Jerrika!"

"And you're letting them."

"What am I 'pose to do? I can't sit up and protect all my spots at the same time."

Jerrika shook her head. Shai was useless. How she ever thought he could take over the streets was beyond her. She looked at his pretty boy ass as he paced the room, looking like a bitch. He was afraid, and fear was the most unattractive thing to Jerrika.

"Call a meeting," she said, "tonight. We need all the generals of GMB to be there."

"And what's a meeting 'pose to accomplish?" Shai asked.

"Just do it. I'll handle the details."

Shai watched her return her attention to her nails and couldn't believe how nonchalant she was. He couldn't help but think how none of this shit would be going down if Duke were by his side. All this time, Shai thought he wanted to sit at the top, but if he knew then what he now knew, he wouldn't have ever let Jerrika talk him into this shit. He wasn't built for it, and it showed.

Jerrika eyed all of the generals of GMB, wondering which one of them were suitable enough to take Shai's place. She could have closed her eyes and played eeny, meeny, miney, moe and chose one, because anyone was better than Shai.

"I heard it was some niggas from Houston," Cristo said as he folded his beefy arms.

"Yeah, I heard the same shit."

"Me too."

"I heard it was some niggas from The Grove," somebody else said.

"I heard it was Ford."

Everyone in the room froze, and Jerrika sat up straight in her chair. She looked at Shai, who looked like he'd swallowed a mouth full of shit.

"Ford?" she asked. "Where you hear that?"

Lou, the one who'd spoken, shrugged. "In the streets. A few niggas said they recognized the way the lil' nigga moved when he ran up in the spot. Said he knew it was Ford as soon as he saw him."

"But they always wear masks!" Shai interjected.

Lou shrugged again. "I'm just repeating what my lil' nigga told me."

Shai's mind was reeling. There was no way it was Ford. Why would he be hitting his spots all of a sudden? Last time he heard, Ford had gone to the Dominican Republic on a dummy mission of revenge. If he was still alive, why would he be in Dallas coming for Shai's neck?

Jerrika was fuming. Unlike Shai, she could list a thousand reasons why Ford would be in Dallas causing trouble for them. She should have killed him when she had the chance! Now they were fucked.

"I don't believe that shit," Shai said with a wave of his hand.

"I do," Jerrika said, dropping a bomb as if it weren't one.

Shai looked at her like she was crazy. Every man in the room stared at her, waiting for her to continue.

"I wasn't going to say nothing," she said slowly, "but I found out a long time ago that Rico Ree, in the Dominican Republic, didn't have anything to do with killing Duke. It was Ford."

The room erupted in shocked gasps, including Shai.

"I wasn't going to ever say anything because I also heard Ford was living in the Dominican Republic because he couldn't step foot back in Dallas after word got out what he'd done."

"Fuckin' right!" Cristo hollered.

"Naw, that don't even sound right," someone else called out. "Ford would never do nothing like, especially not to Duke. He was the most loyal cat I ever knew." A few other people agreed.

"I know what I'm talkin' about!" Jerrika snapped. How dare they second guess her? They worked for her! "And this is the main reason why I didn't wanna say shit, but Ford has forced my hand. If he really is the one hitting our spots, he needs to be taken care of for not only that, but for what he did to Duke." The room was silent as the generals tried to swallow what Jerrika told them.

"I want y'all to put the word on the street that there's a bounty on Ford's head. Two hundred thousand dollars to whoever bodies him," Jerrika said, knowing she'd finally signed

Ford's death certificate. As soon as word got around Dallas that such a high price tag had been placed on Ford's head, every goon and savage from every hood would be after him.

Just like that, her problem had been solved.

CHAPTER TWENTY

Duchess sat on her couch, catching up on the missed episodes of her favorite TV show, when there was a knock at her door. She immediately thought Brian had misplaced his keys until she remembered he was having dinner with a client tonight. She set down the bowl of popcorn she was munching on and got up to answer the door.

When she glanced out the peephole, she saw Ford and someone standing behind him. She couldn't make out the second man but knew he was too tall and bulky to be Gunz. She unlocked the door with a thousand questions running through her head.

Those questions became trapped on the tip of her tongue as soon as she opened the door and saw Duke standing next to Ford. Or was it Demarcus? She couldn't tell.

"Duchess," he said as soon as he laid eyes on her, and in that split second, she *knew*.

She just knew.

Both of her hands went to her mouth as she tried to smother the scream erupting from deep within.

"Can we come in?" Ford asked, but what he was really asking is if she was home alone, and by the way Duchess nodded, he knew the answer.

As soon as Duke stepped foot in Duchess's apartment, he frowned. In the home they'd shared, her closet was bigger than this entire place. He felt an overwhelming sensation of guilt for how life had treated Duchess in his absence. He'd always thought if anything happened to him, she'd be well taken care of. He was sure he'd planned well for it; Duchess's residence proved otherwise.

"Duke?" Duchess was afraid to ask.

"It's me, baby girl." He didn't wait for permission; he ran up to her and engulfed her body in his arms. He wasn't sure how long it'd been since he'd touched her, but by her body's reaction, it had been a long time. He didn't want to let her go and wouldn't have if she hadn't pulled away.

As soon as she pulled away, she slapped him across his face. Duke's head snapped sideways from the force of the slap. He gawked at her as confusion and hurt dilated his pupils.

"Now you wanna show up!" Duchess yelled. She was a ball of mixed emotions. Of course, she was happy to see Duke—she was thrilled, overjoyed even. At the same time, she was hurt and damaged by what Demarcus had done with Duke's life.

"Duch, I'm sorry," Duke said sincerely. "I don't know why any of this happened, but if I had the power to go back and change it, you know I would. Baby, I'm so sorry for everything."

Duchess knew none of this was Duke's fault. He didn't have a hand in anything that had happened to him, but she couldn't help the anger.

"You have no idea what life has been like for me!" She jammed her finger into Duke's chest. "After you died, I lost everything! I even lost the will to fuckin' live! So imagine how it felt when Ford calls and tells me, 'Yo, Duchess, Duke is really alive!' I drop everything and go running to you like I've always done, with no regard to what's best for Duchess."

She cried as she spoke, and Duke wanted to take her into his arms again. He never could stand to see Duchess cry, especially when it was because of him. He tried to reach for her, but she slapped his hands away.

"Don't touch me!"

"Duchess..." Ford tried to interject. This wasn't the reaction he expected, though he understood it.

"Shut up, Ford! You of all people know how I left the Dominican Republic. My heart was shredded into a thousand pieces because he told me to go." She had her finger in Duke's face. "He told me to leave and forget about him!"

"But that wasn't me, Duch. You know that. You know I would never do anything to hurt you," Duke said.

The truth was, Duchess did know that. She knew as sure as she knew her name, Duke would rather die than hurt her. She was just so angry at the entire situation and didn't know what else to do with the wrath other than to throw it at Duke.

"I wish none of this shit happened, baby girl," Duke said, his voice border lining defeat. "I woke up three days ago like my bachelor party had just happened. I didn't know who the fuck the woman I married was. I didn't even recognize my own son."

Duchess blinked back the tears as she remembered Demarcus's family. "Where are they? Are they here?" She looked toward her front door as if she expected them to walk through at any moment.

"No," Duke said. "I left them in the DR." He didn't bother expounding on the fact that he planned on returning for his son. He may not have remembered conceiving him or his birth, but Duke would never pretend he didn't exist. As far as Auri, she was dead to him. The only reason she was still breathing was because of Rico's protection. Otherwise, for what she'd done to Duke, he'd killed her with his bare hands.

Duchess wiped her face and shook her head. She laughed and threw her hands in the air. "I don't know what to say, Duke! Everything is fucked up."

Duke didn't care how much she fought him. There was no way he could witness her in so much agony and not comfort her. He wrapped his arms around her and held onto her as tightly as he could, her body as familiar to him as his own. Time and distance may have separated them, but their bond was bulletproof. He held her as their broken connection began to mend. The rich history of a love that didn't get the chance to die—could never die—rustled between them.

Duchess melted in Duke's embrace. How many nights had she prayed for this very moment? How many nights had she cried herself to sleep, knowing it would never happen? She couldn't fight Duke even if she had the strength to do so. She loved this man with the very breath in her lungs, and as he held her, she felt their souls embrace and connect once again.

She wasn't mad at Duke. She was mad at what happened to force them apart, mad at the two years wasted that they could have built together. As he held her, he healed every moment shattered by his absence.

He placed kisses on her forehead and whispered promises that he'd die before breaking. "I love you, Duchess. I'm so sorry, baby girl. I'm here now. I'm here, and I'm never leaving you again."

Duchess lifted her head and looked into his eyes. This was really happening. This was her Duke. At the moment their eyes connected, nothing and no one else mattered. Her lips begged for his, and he heard the unspoken request and placed his mouth on top of hers.

Duchess kissed Duke with the hunger of a starving woman. Their kiss was intense, powerful, and a reunion two years in the making.

Duke grabbed both sides of Duchess's face as he kissed her. He didn't want to pull away, but he did. With his hands still on her face, he made sure she was looking at him. "I need you to know it wasn't me that married that woman, Duch. You know that wasn't me. You know I wouldn't ever..."

"I know, baby," she whispered, tears steady falling down her face.

Duke planned to kiss every single one of them away. If it took the rest of his life, he would spend it erasing the pain he'd caused Duchess.

Ford cleared his throat. Duke and Duchess had been so wrapped into each other that they hadn't heard the sound of keys entering the door. Ford's hand was on his pistol, fully expecting Brian to enter the house on some dumb shit upon seeing his woman in the arms of another man. However, Brian hadn't reacted in the way Ford knew he would, had it been him in this situation.

Brian dropped the bouquet of flowers that were in his hand, and his mouth fell at the same time. He knew what he saw, but it was still hard to believe his eyes.

"Duchess?" He'd called her name at least five more times, but she hadn't heard him and hadn't wanted to.

Ford cleared his throat again. This time, Duke looked at him, questioning why he was interrupting them. Ford shot his head in the direction of Brian.

Duchess jumped back as soon as she saw Brian standing in the doorway. The pain of betrayal contorted his facial features.

"Brian!" She didn't know what else to say.

Duke allowed Duchess to jump out of his arms, but he wouldn't let her stay out of them for long. He sized Brian up. So this was her man? He chuckled because this had to be a joke. There was no way in hell his Duchess was laid up with such a square ass, cornball nigga. The humor of the situation quickly melted as Duke thought about this man's hands touching what belonged to him. His fists involuntarily balled.

Ford watched the change in his brother's body language and knew it was time for them to go. "Uh, let's get out of here, bro."

Brian's eyes barely registered Duke. They were stuck on Duchess... his woman... his fiancée. She wore his fucking ring while her lips were on this man! The burning heat of betrayal crept up Brian's neck.

Duke continued studying Brian, in full disbelief that this was the man Duchess was prepared to marry. He couldn't put his finger on it, but there was something familiar about this nigga. Duke's mind was cloudy and full of a lot of shit that he couldn't remember, yet there was a nagging familiarity about Brian in the back of his mind.

"Let's go," Ford repeated.

"I ain't going nowhere until Duchess tells me to," Duke proclaimed.

"Duke, please," Duchess said against her will. Nothing in her wanted to see Duke walk out of her apartment, but she couldn't just do Brian any kind of way. He'd never done anything to deserve what was happening. "Please go. We'll talk later."

Duke looked at Duchess as if she spoke another language, and he didn't move.

"Come on, Duke." Ford tried to grab Duke's arm and lead him toward the door because if they stayed a minute longer, shit was going to pop off.

As expected, Duke snatched away from Ford. "Naw, fuck that! Duchess, tell this nigga what it is." He fully expected Duchess to tell Brian to kick rocks. He was back now. They were supposed to pick up right where they left off. He didn't give a fuck if it had been two years or ten years. He was back to claim what was rightfully his, what he'd never given away.

"Duke..." Duchess said, her voice pleading with him.

"Please."

Duke felt like Duchess had just pulled out a knife and stuck it in his chest. Reason told him it'd been two years, and she'd built a relationship with this nigga and couldn't just dismiss him that easily, but Duke couldn't listen to reason. To him, it'd only been three days since he left Duchess. She was still his fiancée, his woman, his entire world.

Now, it felt as if she was choosing this lame over him, and Duke couldn't take it. "Fuck it then." He stormed out of the apartment, his shoulder bumping against Brian's as he fumed past him.

Ford didn't say a word as he followed Duke out of the apartment. He wanted to be long gone before Duchess and Brian began what was sure to be an awkward ass conversation.

CHAPTER TWENTY ONE

Auri wasn't sure what she'd been waiting on. Day in and day out, she stared at her phone, thinking Demarcus would call her. She had to constantly remind herself that there was no Demarcus anymore. Duke had returned and wanted nothing to do with her.

She would never forgive Rico for telling Duke everything from how she found him in the hospital to how she'd led him to believe he was someone else. The murderous rage she'd seen in Duke's eyes expressed he wasn't anything like Demarcus and would never forgive her.

The following day, he returned to America, and she hadn't heard from him since. It was a hard pill to swallow and a bitter truth to accept. She was going to be a single mother. She had to return back to the club in order to feed Levi and herself. What made things worse was the blaring truth that she'd done this to herself.

Ten days... it'd been ten days since Duke got his memory back and left her. It was over for them, but she'd held out hope that he wouldn't abandon his seed. Silly of her to hang onto that small thread of hope. She looked at her son and began to cry. She'd failed him.

Just as quickly as she'd started crying, she stopped. Since Duke had returned and stole her happily ever after, he didn't deserve one with his fiancée back in Dallas. Oh, fuck that! Auri wouldn't go back to the club fucking and sucking to make ends meet. She didn't create Levi by herself, so why should she take care of him by herself?

She'd given Duke ten whole days to do right by her. It was obvious he wasn't going to do that, so the ball was now in her court. She jumped out of bed and ran into her closet to pack a few bags. Duke may not ever return to the Dominican Republic, so Auri was going to Dallas, Texas.

"Duchess?" Brian said, still waiting for an explanation for what he'd walked into.

Duchess ran her hands through her hair. In the matter of an hour, her entire world had been flipped upside down for the third time. She could barely gather her thoughts, let alone have this conversation with Brian.

"You wanna tell me what the fuck is going on?" Brian demanded, losing patience.

"That was Duke," she said as if he didn't know.

Brian could count on one hand the amount of times he'd lost his cool, but if Duchess didn't stop playing with him, tonight was going to be one of those times.

"He got his memory back," she said. "He doesn't remember anything from the last two years. To him, he's just left the DR for his bachelor party. It's like no time has passed."

"And? What the fuck does that have to do with us? We're getting married, Duchess! Remember that? You're wearing my ring for fuck's sake!"

Duchess looked at the engagement ring on her finger. She

wouldn't tell Brian right now, but there was no way in hell she was going through with their wedding.

"Don't tell me you're having second thoughts!" Brian shouted as if he could read her mind. "Don't let him waltz up in here after playing house with another woman in the DR and give you second thoughts about us." Brian's voice was damn near pleading.

He walked up to Duchess and tried to wrap his arms around her, but she stepped out of his reach. Her skin still tingled from Duke's touch, and she didn't want the sensation to end or be contaminated by Brian.

"Don't do this to me, Duchess," Brian said. "Please, don't do this to *us*."

Duchess looked at him and saw the pain she caused him. She never wanted to hurt Brian. She did love him; she just wasn't in love with him. She should have never said yes when he proposed. She should have never given him the false impression that she was ready to move on from Duke. Now she had to break his heart.

"You know what?" Brian held his hand in the air, "You're obviously confused, so I'm gonna give you some space and time to come to your senses." He stalked past Duchess into her bedroom where he gathered a few of his belongings.

He walked to the front door with his things in his arms. He wasn't going to say another word to Duchess but stopped and turned around before grabbing the doorknob. "I'm gonna give you a few days to get your thoughts together. I'm not gonna wait forever, Duchess."

She didn't try to stop him when he walked out of the door and slammed it behind him.

"Gunz? Is that you, nigga?"

Gunz froze in place, and his hand went straight to his pistol. He was tired of being held up in his apartment, and the one time he decided to venture out, he was recognized. Ford was gonna be pissed!

"Gunz?" the voice behind him repeated.

Gunz slowly turned around. He was a few feet from his car. He'd almost made it back before being spotted. Now he was gonna have to kill whoever this was in this gas station's parking lot.

"I knew that was yo' ass!" the young boy said before running up to Gunz and embracing him warmly.

Gunz immediately recognized him as KP, a member of GMB. They'd always been cool, so Gunz let his guard down.

"Aye, KP. What's good, my nigga?"

"You tell me! Where the hell you been hiding? Niggas thought you was dead or some shit."

"Naw, I ain't dead."

"I can see that!" KP laughed. He looked Gunz up and down and then shook his head as if he couldn't believe his eyes. "Where you been?"

"I been around," Gunz said.

"Same ol' Gunz." KP chuckled. He looked toward Gunz's car for Tommy. He knew the twins rarely traveled without the other. "Say, where Tommy at?"

Gunz flinched. "Oh, he at the house," he lied. KP had always been cool, but Gunz wasn't about to confide in him.

"Say, y'all trying to get in on that bounty?" KP said, rubbing his hands together.

"What bounty?"

"Oh yeah, I forgot! That is ya mans." KP immediately regretted opening his mouth. He knew Gunz's temper could turn deadly at a moment's notice and hoped he hadn't just said something to get himself killed.

"What the hell you talkin' 'bout, KP?"

KP scratched the back of his head while looking around the parking lot for reinforcements. He reluctantly continued. "Shai nem got a bounty on Ford's head."

Gunz almost dropped the plastic bag of junk food he held. "Shai did what? Why?"

KP leaned in closer to Gunz as if someone was listening in to their conversation. "Word is he was the one offed Duke and tried to put the shit on that Dominican boss Rico."

Gunz's face curled in confusion. That story didn't even make sense. Ford wasn't even on the boat when Duke was killed. He knew that for a fact, but no one in Dallas knew that. They believed any and everything Shai told them. He had the hood thinking Ford had gone against the grain and murked his own brother! Gunz was livid.

"How much?"

"Two hunned thou," KP said with a large grin. That kind of money would change his life completely; he wanted so bad to be the trigger man. Even though he knew Ford's reputation was something deadly, that kind of money would make any man take the risk. Plus, Ford had it coming. A nigga who would kill his own blood needed to be taken out.

Gunz couldn't believe his ears. Somehow, Shai had gotten wind that Ford was back in the city. He knew Shai was pussy but not this big of one. He didn't have the balls to come at Ford himself, so he put a hit on his head that was so large a nigga's own momma would turn on him.

"Damn!" Gunz said.

"I know, right!" KP said, mistaking Gunz's enthusiasm. He rubbed his hands together again. "Niggas in wildin' out here for that kinda bread."

Gunz winced. His man was a walking target out here and didn't even know it.

"Yo, hop in the car with me," Gunz said, motioning toward his Caprice.

"For what?" KP asked, his earlier suspicion returning.

"Just take a ride with me," Gunz said, then he forced a smile to show himself friendly and not a threat.

"A'ight." KP hopped in Gunz's car, thinking about how sweet it would be to come up on that two hundred thousand dollars.

"I'm gonna kill that nigga!" Duke yelled.

Ford looked over at his brother and shook his head. "Man, your beef ain't with that man, bro. He ain't do shit to you. He didn't know you existed when he got with Duchess."

Duke knew his brother was talking sense, but he was being irrational and didn't want to hear Ford. "Fuck that! That's my woman!"

Ford shook his head again. "We need to be thinkin' about Shai's ass. It's his fault this shit is happening anyway."

That, Duke could agree with. "Oh, his ass is grass too."

Ford pulled up to a red light. He was in Lewisville, a part of town he rarely visited, so his surroundings were unfamiliar. He peeped the dark tinted windows on a van that pulled up next to him but paid it no mind. He was too busy trying to talk sense to a rambling Duke.

"I'm gonna murder every fuckin' body involved in this bullshit!" Duke yelled as he counted them off on his fingers. "Shai, Auri, that hoe ass nigga Duchess laid up with." He stopped and looked over at Ford who laughed at him. At the same time, in his peripheral, he spotted the doors flying open to the van next to them at the light. About four dudes hopped out, all armed with assault weapons. "Go!" Duke hollered at the same time they opened fire.

He saw it before it could happen, before the first bullet crashed into the driver's window, before it could enter Ford's head.

Ford didn't even look to see what the threat was. He heard the urgency in Duke's voice and smashed his foot on the gas, running the red light. The sound of gunfire erupted behind them as they sped off.

"What the fuck!" Ford hollered as he looked in his rearview and got a glimpse of four men dressed in all black, hopping back into the van.

"I don't know," Duke said as he retrieved a gun from underneath the passenger seat, "but they fucked with me at the wrong time."

Ford kept his eyes on the road as Duke opened the large sunroof. Duke didn't feel a trace of fear, even as he saw the van speeding toward them. He took aim at the driver and let off four shots. Seconds later, the van began erratically moving. Duke's aim was flawless. He'd hit driver in the forehead, causing him to lose control of the van that was driving so fast it was inevitable it would crash into the street pole less than a few feet away. The pole seemed to split the van in half. Duke didn't have to be there when the firetruck and ambulance arrived to know there would be no survivors.

Ford pulled up into his apartment and was glad to see Gunz's car parked outside. Him and Duke raced up the stairs to the third floor apartment. They froze when they saw Gunz sitting on the couch, passing a blunt to KP.

KP dropped the blunt as soon as he saw Ford run into the apartment. He jumped from the couch before it could burn through his jeans. He tried to wrap his head around the fact Ford had just walked through the door and he didn't have a gun to make good on the bounty, when his eyes locked on Duke.

The fucking Duke of Dallas!

"Wa-wait. What's going on?" KP heard himself say but he didn't realize he'd even spoken.

"Sit down, KP," Gunz said calmly. "I'ma tell you everything, but I need you to sit down and chill out first."

"Chill out!" KP screamed. He pointed to Duke. "Nigga! Duke just walked into your apartment, and you tellin' me to chill out. A fuckin' ghost is standing right there, and you want me to chill out?" KP was seconds from making a run for it.

"I ain't a ghost, KP," Duke said. He'd always been fond of KP and knew his character was solid, so he understood why Gunz brought him there.

KP's eyes watered. If Duke wasn't a ghost, then he wasn't dead. He looked at Gunz. "What the fuck, man?"

"Take a seat, man," Gunz said, and this time KP did.

Gunz explained everything to KP whose eyes got wider and wider as the story progressed. It was then KP's turn to tell Duke and Ford about the bounty on Ford's head.

"Shit!" Ford couldn't sit still. "Niggas came at us right

before we made it here. They just ran up on us and started shooting! I'm a walking meal ticket out here!"

"Calm down," Duke said, even though his brother wasn't listening.

KP stared at Duke in awe. He'd heard the whole story, but he still looked at Duke as if he'd stepped out of a grave. Duke was like a myth, and once the streets found out he was alive, he would be an urban legend all over Dallas.

"KP, we need you to help us get to Shai," Duke said.

KP's head resembled a bobblehead toy. "Anything. Just say the word."

Duke smiled. He could taste the revenge already, and it was as sweet as sugar.

CHAPTER
TWENTY TWO

"What do you mean the wedding is off?" Pamela couldn't believe what Duchess was telling her.

"It's off, Momma."

"Why?" Pamela sounded like she was on the verge of tears, as if it were her own wedding being called off. "What did you do?"

Duchess's head snapped in her mother's direction. "What did I do?" She could barely believe her mother's reaction, but then again, yes she could.

"Yes!" Pamela yelled. "I know *you* had to do something! Brian loves you! He would never call the wedding off."

All Duchess could do was laugh. Even though she hadn't told Brian yet, she was telling Pamela the wedding was off. She was finally ready to admit out loud what she already knew in her heart. "I don't wanna marry Brian. I never did."

"Why? He's perfect!"

"No one is perfect."

"Well, he's a lot better than Duke!"

Duchess couldn't even get upset at her mother. She didn't try to hide how she felt about Duke, so Duchess stopped holding it against her.

"Whatever," she said, heading for the front door. This conversation was over. "I love Duke. I don't love Brian."

Pamela shook her head. "Duke is gone, Duchess! When are you going to let him go?"

"No, Momma. Duke is back. He's back in Dallas and remembers everything. I can't live a lie with Brian now that Duke is back."

Pamela felt like Duchess had just slapped her across her face. She hadn't expected that bombshell about Duke. In fact, she would have rather heard anything other than Duke returning with his memory intact.

"But he has a wife and a kid..." Pamela was grasping for straws.

"Their marriage wasn't legal, so technically, she was never his wife. As far as his son, Duke is going to be a father to Levi."

"So you're gonna deal with baby momma drama for the rest of your life?" Pamela curled up her face, illustrating the disgust she felt. She wanted so much more for Duchess, but it seemed like Duchess wanted to lay in the gutter with her drug dealing boyfriend and play step momma to his bastard kid.

Duchess hadn't really thought much about where and how Auri would fit into their lives. She hadn't thought much about Auri at all since Duke reappeared.

"You were doing so well with your life, Duchess. Duke comes around like a cancer that kills everything in its path, and once again, you're throwing everything away."

Duchess swore she wouldn't let her mother's words get to her, but everything Pamela said was so hateful. Duchess stood to leave.

"Bye, Momma."

Pamela sucked her teeth but didn't try to stop Duchess. Duchess expected this reaction from her mother, but she'd wished for something different. She hoped, for once, her mother would understand; for once, she would realize her heart belonged to Duke and forever would. She left her childhood home, unsure if she would ever return again.

As Duchess drove to the bakery, she thought about Auri and what Pamela had said. She'd never met Auri, but Duchess already knew what kind of chick she was, so she knew without a doubt Auri was going to be the baby momma from hell.

Meanwhile, Auri and Levi were leaving DFW International Airport in an Uber. She didn't know where to find Duke but knew just like in the Dominican Republic, his name held major weight, so it wouldn't be hard to locate him. She didn't know what she would do once she saw him again. She hadn't thought that far in advance. Since he'd walked out of her life, it felt like she was losing her mind. Some days, she missed Demarcus so much that she felt physical pain. Other days, she was on some *if I can't have you no one can* shit. She wasn't herself. Everything that was once so perfect had gone to shit, and Auri looked to make someone pay.

Someone had to be held responsible for ruining her happily ever after.

Not too many people knew where Shai laid his head these days. He knew firsthand people couldn't be trusted, so he didn't put shit past anyone. He was suspicious of everyone he came in contact with, even members of GMB, but when KP called and told him he had info on Ford, Shai went against his own instinct and invited the young boy to his crib.

He didn't tell Jerrika about this meeting. They weren't even on speaking terms these days. After the stunt she'd pulled at the meeting with the GMB generals, Shai didn't have shit to say to her. She hadn't thought about how this new story would make Shai look. Most of their clique thought Shai had been on the yacht with Duke when Rico killed him. Jerrika's new story contradicted that. Luckily, no one had called them out on it yet.

Shai wasn't sure if Ford was really behind the robberies of his spots, but of course he was sure Ford hadn't killed Duke. That didn't mean he gave two fucks about the hit Jerrika put on Ford's head though. He'd already written Ford off when he went back to the Dominican Republic on some revenge shit. Shai had been completely disinterested with the entire situation until he received the call from KP saying he had proof that Ford was behind the robberies. Shai needed to see if this proof checked out.

At seven o'clock on the dot, KP rang Shai's doorbell as planned. Shai answered the door holding a glass of Hennessy. His nerves were on edge, and he needed something to relax. What was supposed to be one glass turned into five, so Shai was good and drunk by the time KP arrived.

"Damn, KP, you a punctual ass nigga!" Shai said after inviting KP into his home. He looked at the time on his watch and shook his head. "I like that you respect my time by being on time."

KP was amazed by the size of Shai's crib. Shai was really on his boss shit. His house resembled something KP had only seen on TV. Now, he knew why few people knew where Shai laid his head. If he was living this lavishly, he wouldn't want niggas to know either.

KP eyed the security cameras in the foyer as he walked past them. He'd expected that. What he hadn't predicted was how easy it was to get into Shai's home. He'd anticipated at least one or two members of GMB guarding Shai's front door. However, Shai didn't have anyone protecting him. He was either confident that he'd never be found or a gotdamn fool. KP couldn't tell which one.

Shai led KP into the living room. "You want something to drink?"

"Yeah, I'll take a beer," KP said. He was about to start running his mouth and needed something to wet his throat before he started singing.

Shai grabbed a can of beer from the stainless steel refrigerator and handed it to KP before joining him on the couch. "So, KP, tell me what you found out."

KP took a long swig from his beer. "Ford is the one who has been hitting ya spots, but he hasn't been doing it alone. That nigga Gunz been helping him. And probably Tommy too, but I ain't seen Tommy."

Shai was drunk but not drunk enough to not take notice of the names KP dropped. He sat up straight on the sofa. "How you know this shit, KP?"

"'Cause I ran into Gunz the other day at the gas station. We went back to his crib to shoot the shit, and he told me. Said him and Ford been back in Dallas for six months hitting all yo' spots."

Shai shook his head. "What the fuck! Why? Did he tell you why?"

"You ain't gonna believe this, Shai. He said 'cause Ford thinks you killed Duke."

The Hennessy suddenly tasted like buttermilk in Shai's mouth. He set his glass on the coffee table and tried to keep himself from getting sick all over his white sofa. "He said wh-what?"

"Said you killed that nigga Duke and blamed it on Rico Ree," KP repeated. He looked around the house, wondering if they were alone. "Say Shai, anyone else here?"

"Naw, ain't nobody here but us. You ain't gotta worry about that. Plus, I appreciate you for bringing this to me before putting it on the streets. For that, you got my protection."

KP had to bite his tongue to keep from laughing. Shai couldn't even protect his traps, so Shai sure couldn't protect him from Ford, Gunz, and Duke. "I appreciate your offer for protection, Shai, but as soon as I leave here, I'm getting the fuck outta dodge. I got an auntie that stay in Atlanta, and that's where I'm headed. I was hoping you could bless me with a few dollars for this valuable information I'm bringing you."

"Of course, of course." Shai nodded his head. "I got you. What else Gunz tell you?"

KP pulled his vibrating cell from his pocket. "Hol' up. This my worrisome ass baby mama. Let me text her back right quick." KP sent the text before looking back at Shai. "It ain't what he told me that's gonna fuck your head up, Shai. It's what he showed me. So we sitting on the couch getting high and shit, and guess who comes strolling through the front door?"

Shai didn't feel like playing the guessing game right now. "Who, nigga?"

"Duke muthafuckin Kingston!"

Shai knew for sure now he was about to ruin his couch and the matching white rug beneath his feet. The room began spinning, and sweat trickled down his forehead. His stomach did a few somersaults as nausea hit him strong. "Wait. I thought you just said Gunz said that I killed Duke. How could Duke walk through the door if I killed him?"

"That's why I knew it was some bullshit! They sitting up here saying you was plotting on Duke and killed him, but the nigga come walking through the door looking untouched!"

Shai's tongue felt like it had doubled in size; it stuck to the roof of his mouth.

"That nigga Duke is alive, Shai!" KP said, still unable to really believe it himself.

"You sure?"

"Hell yeah, I'm sure! I know Duke when I see him. He chopped it up with me for a while and then tried to talk me into turning on you. I played it off like I was down, but you know I would never cross GMB like that," KP said before finishing the last of his beer.

"I appreciate that, KP. It's hard as hell to find real loyalty like that these days," Shai said. He tried to think fast, but his drunken brain moved in slow motion. If he were to believe anything KP had just said, he was in real trouble right now. It was only a matter of time before Duke came for him.

"Say Shai, I need to get up outta here. You think you can run me that bread now so I can be on my way?" KP asked, nervously looking around the room as if he expected someone to jump out at any moment.

Shai debated if he should pay KP or just put a bullet in his head. If it wasn't for what he'd just told him, Shai would be walking around blind to Duke's reappearance, so he decided against killing the young boy. "Let me run upstairs and get that for you. Sit tight, my nigga."

Shai got up on wobbly legs and walked up the stairs for a few stacks to give KP, all the while trying to figure out his next move. How the hell could Duke be alive? And what took him so long to come back?

Shai grabbed five stacks from his safe and made his way back downstairs. KP sat in the same spot he'd left him. Shai tossed the money at him. "Don't repeat anything you've said tonight to anyone. Go to Georgia like you planned and take this conversation to the grave, alright?"

"Bet," KP said as he flipped through the rubber banded

money. He looked up at Shai. "The shit ain't true, is it?" He had to know before he left.

"What?" Shai asked.

"About you trying to kill Duke."

"Hell naw!" Shai said, but he didn't even try to make it sound convincing.

"You a bitch ass lie," a familiar voice said from behind him.

Shai felt his bladder empty itself. The warm liquid ran down his thighs and legs, wetting his jeans in the process.

"Eeeew! He pissing himself!" KP said before bursting into laughter. He'd stood and pocketed the money Shai had given him. His part was done, and now he was about to be on his way.

Shai felt the sensation of cold steel to the back of his head, and tears welled in his eyes.

"You always was a pussy," Duke growled. He held the gun steady to Shai's head, savoring the taste of his fear.

Gunz and Ford came from the back of the house. "We couldn't find it," Ford said, referring to the safe where they knew Shai had money and dope stashed.

"If this nigga is the jealous ass serpent that I think he is, then he has a safe upstairs in the media room just like I had," Duke said. "Ain't that right, Shai? You always did want to be me, huh?"

"Man, Duke, it ain't even like that!" Shai protested, tears flowing freely down his face. "I didn't want to do it. I swear. It was Jerrika! It was all her idea! You know how that bitch can be. She got in my head and just wouldn't stay out my ear with the bullshit!"

Gunz and Ford exchanged looks. They'd had their suspicions about Jerrika, and now it had been confirmed.

"You let a bitch talk you into crossing your brother!" Duke hollered before hitting Shai in the back of his head with the butt of the gun. He was enraged, but even worse, he was hurt, a deadly combination.

Shai fell to the floor, bright red blood spewing across the white shag rug. Seconds later, he emptied his stomach all over that same rug. He was about to die, and he knew it. All he could hope for now was that Duke would make it quick and as painless as possible.

Duke kicked Shai while shaking his head in disgust. He looked so pitiful that Duke almost felt bad for what was about to happen. Then he thought about the two years of his life that he'd lost because of this nigga and kicked him again.

Ford and Gunz went upstairs in search of Shai's safe. Sure enough, they found it in the media room behind a poster, just as Duke had said. It was a poor attempt at hiding the obvious, and they'd found it within seconds of entering the room. Shai had tried to copy Duke, but Ford knew damn well his brother's safe hadn't been so sloppily hidden.

They began immediately emptying Shai of his goods while laughing at the screams of torture that they heard all the way upstairs.

"Duke giving it to his ass!" Gunz laughed, itching to join Duke in the torture.

"Sounds like it," Ford agreed.

"Can you believe that bitch Jerrika?" Gunz asked with a shake of his head.

All Ford could do was shake his head also. Nothing surprised him anymore. The game was grimy, and no one could be trusted.

Downstairs, Shai was on his back as he looked up at Duke, pleading for his life, even though it was useless to do so. What he'd done was punishable by death, and Duke had sentenced him to the death penalty.

Duke couldn't believe his life had been turned inside out by a nigga he called his brother. Anger caused him to go to that dark place where wrath controlled his limbs. At one point, Shai stopped fighting back. He stopped screaming, but Duke still threw blow after blow fueled by fury. He'd completely blacked out and beat Shai until he lay motionless in the middle of the floor.

By the time Ford and Gunz made it back downstairs, Shai was dead. Duke had killed him with his bare hands.

CHAPTER TWENTY-THREE

Jerrika kissed Cristo goodbye before hopping into her Bentley coupe and heading home. If she had been unsure before, the sex tonight had convinced her. Cristo would be the one to take Shai's place as the man in her life and head of GMB. He was everything Shai wasn't, and Jerrika couldn't wait to get rid of Shai. She hadn't decided just how she'd do it but knew death was the only way Shai would let her and Cristo take over Dallas.

She turned the volume up on her radio and sang loudly all the way home. She was riding on a cloud from the multiple orgasms that Cristo had given her. Shai could never!

She pulled into their driveway and got out of her car, still singing to herself. As soon as she entered the home, a rank smell hit her nostrils. "Eeew, what the fuck is that smell?"

She stepped out of her high heels, not wanting to walk through her home in them. She didn't get halfway through the foyer before her eyes zeroed in on Shai's body in the middle of the living room floor. The rug beneath his body was drenched in so much blood and no longer looked as if it once had been white. There was so much blood spattered all over the walls and couch. It looked like a massacre had occurred in her living room.

Jerrika gagged as she walked closer to Shai's body. The putrid smell of piss, shit, and blood got stronger the closer she got. She covered her mouth to keep the vomit down. She even began to cry. Yes, just minutes earlier, she was planning his death in her mind, but seeing Shai like this made her emotional. He was literally beat beyond recognition.

Jerrika didn't know if the assailant was still in her house or not. She opened her clutch purse and pulled out the .22 she kept with her at all times. Her heart raced, and her nerves were all over the place. She listened for someone, but the house was completely silent. She walked throughout the house with her gun pointed, ready to pull the trigger at any sign of motion. She thoroughly checked each and every room of the large house. When she made it upstairs to the media room, her heart fell to the soles of her feet. She knew before entering the safe that it had been cleaned out.

Sure enough, the safe was completely empty.

"Shit!" Jerrika screamed with all the force of her vocal cords. She ran back downstairs and grabbed her cell to call Cristo.

"Don't touch anything," he instructed as soon as she'd told him what she walked into. "I'm gonna send dem boys over there to clean everything." He exhaled loudly as he wondered who the hell killed Shai. Shit was about to get funky in Dallas now. "Who you think did this?"

"I don't know!" Jerrika shrieked. At the moment, she was less worried about who killed Shai and more about the fact that they'd left her destitute. She always knew keeping their life's savings in one spot was a bad idea, but Shai wouldn't listen. For some reason, he'd been convinced the safe hidden in the media room was genius and no one could ever find it. Now, Shai was dead, and she was dead broke.

"Think, Jerrika!" Cristo said. "There has to be someone who knew where you and Shai live."

Jerrika couldn't think of one person who had their new address, but she could name at least a hundred people who wanted Shai dead. She looked at his badly beaten corpse and winced. Whoever did this beat him with such venom that it had to be personal. This was beyond robbery.

This was revenge.

"It had to be Ford," she said.

"Ford!" Cristo yelled. He hadn't really believed that shit about Ford being back in Dallas or having anything to do with Duke's death. Now Jerrika was putting Shai's death on Ford as well. If she hadn't been laid up with him at the time of Shai's death, Cristo would have suspected that she'd killed Shai herself. Other than the fact that she was fucking him behind Shai's back, there was something about Jerrika that Cristo thought was suspect.

"Yes, Cristo. I said Ford! He is the only person who would have done some shit like this! Shai wasn't shot! He was beat to death!"

"Beat to death?" Cristo repeated. That further let him know Ford hadn't been behind this; Ford wasn't built like that. He was all about gunplay.

Jerrika heard the doubt in Cristo's voice, and it pissed her off. She wanted to curse him out, but fuck it! She didn't need Cristo to believe her. She *knew* Ford was behind this. Somehow, he'd found out what really happened to Duke and came here for vengeance. Chills ran down Jerrika's spine. If Ford had found out about Shai's part in the plot to kill Duke, Ford had to also know that she was involved as well. She looked around the house, suddenly afraid to be there.

"I have to get out of here."

"Wait. I just sent my peoples over there."

"I don't wanna stay here, Cristo!" she whined but then realized she didn't have anywhere else to go. All she had to her name was a couple hundred dollars in her wallet, so staying at a hotel tonight was out of the question. That two hundred dollars would have to stretch until she decided her next move.

She'd be damned if she called any of those hoes that pretended to be friends with her. They only went clubbing with her to get in free and be associated with GMB. She couldn't call Billie or Duchess because she'd completely played them both.

She was fucked.

"Can I come stay with you tonight?" Jerrika asked Cristo, knowing he'd jump at the chance of fucking her again.

"Uhhh... I don't think so. My ol' lady coming back into town tonight."

"Your ol' lady?" Jerrika was confused. Since when was Cristo married? She couldn't remember ever seeing him with a woman. Then again, Jerrika had been so self-absorbed and wouldn't have noticed if he came around with a woman hanging off his arm.

"Yeah. Tamika," he said as if Jerrika should have known his wife's name.

Jerrika wanted to beg Cristo, but her pride wouldn't allow Her. Even with her life on the line, she couldn't gravel and beg a nigga to let her spend the night. Even though Ford knew exactly where to find her, she would just have to sleep here tonight. She didn't have anywhere else to go.

Sleeping with one eye open was better than sleeping on the streets. If Jerrika didn't come up with a game plan soon, that's exactly where she'd end up. She was going to stay in this house until the landlord put her out, which wouldn't be long, seeing as she no longer had the money to pay next month's mortgage.

Damn it!

Just an hour ago, life was good, and Jerrika was riding on a cloud. Now she wondered if she'd even have a roof over her head next month.

Auri wasn't running into any luck finding Duke. People looked at her as if she were crazy when she asked about him. Everyone in Dallas seemed to still believe he was dead. Auri was running low on hope that she'd ever find him. This trip was turning out to be a waste of time, an epic failure.

Auri sat in a popular diner in Far North Dallas. She'd been told that anybody who was somebody ate here. Surely, someone here would be able to help her. When her waitress approached her table to deliver the food she'd ordered, Auri decided to take a different approach with her search because asking about Duke was getting her nowhere.

"Excuse me, do you know where I can find a woman named Duchess?" Auri asked the young, copper-skinned waitress as she set the plate of food in front of her.

The waitress lifted her perfectly arched eyebrow. It'd been a minute since she heard that name. "You talkin' about Duke's girl?"

Auri bit back the emotion threatening to erupt inside of her. "Yeah, her."

"Damn, I ain't heard that name in a minute," the waitress said. "She and Duke used to always be out and about around the city, but ever since he died, Duchess been real lowkey."

Auri's shoulders fell. Another dead end. "Do you know anyone who might know where I can find her?"

The waitress shook her head. "I'm sorry, sweetie, I don't. Nobody really sees Duchess anymore." She turned her attention to Levi, who was getting restless in Auri's lap. "Your son is so cute."

"Thanks," Auri replied dryly. She'd flown all the way to the States on a dummy mission. She couldn't believe she was in the same city as Duke and couldn't even find him. The disappointment she felt was written all over her face.

The waitress felt bad that she couldn't help Auri because it was obvious that she was desperate to find Duchess for whatever reason. She smiled sympathetically at Auri before walking away to tend to her next customer.

Auri sat in the diner for another hour before deciding it was time to leave. Just as she gathered her things to leave, someone tapped her on the shoulder. She turned around to see a short, chubby, light-skinned woman wearing a waitress uniform.

"I heard you was looking for Duchess," the woman said.

"Yeah, I am." Auri's eyes lit up. "Do you know where I can find her?"

"I know exactly where she lives 'cause my cousin delivered a pizza to her place last week," the girl said while taking notice of the designer shoes on Auri's feet, the diamonds in her ears, and the fat ass carat on her ring finger. "How much you willing to pay for the address?"

Auri knew she was being hustled, but at this point, it didn't matter.

She needed that address.

Duchess felt like a teenager going on her first date. Duke had called her earlier and asked if it was alright for him to stop by. He'd given her two days to get over the shock of his return—to get rid of Brian.

Duchess waited with bated breath for his arrival. He'd taken up residence in her mind these last couple of days. She couldn't concentrate in class. She burned cookies and donuts at work. She was a mess.

With a hand that was shaky due to her nerves, she lit the candles on top of her small dining table. She wanted to surprise Duke tonight with a home cooked meal by candlelight. She didn't expect to jump headfirst back into a relationship with Duke, because so much had changed. At the same time, she couldn't imagine her life without him. Maybe they could take things slow and if it felt right, fall back right where they left off.

When her doorbell rung, she almost jumped out of her skin. She checked her appearance in the mirror before rushing to open it. As soon as the door opened, she inhaled enough air to overfill her lungs. Duke was the only man who had that kind of power over Duchess. He stood smiling at her, his beautiful dimples on full display. His cocky swag was on ten, and best of all, he knew exactly who Duchess was.

She hugged him and gave him a quick kiss on the cheek before inviting him inside. The smell of his cologne lingered in the air long after he walked past her, turning on the faucet between her legs.

"All this for me?" Duke asked as soon as he saw the candlelit dinner set out for him.

Duchess blushed. She wasn't sure why she felt shy all of a sudden. She could barely meet Duke's eye contact.

"You didn't have to go all out like this," Duke said as he closed the distance between them. He wrapped his arms around her waist. "Damn, it's good seeing you again, baby girl."

Duchess smiled at the nickname that only Duke called

her. She never thought she'd hear it from his lips again, so hearing it now sounded so melodic.

When Duke noticed Duchess stiffening in his arms, he released her. He wasn't sure what that was about, but the last thing he wanted to do was make her uncomfortable in any way. He had to keep reminding himself that, for her, it'd been two years, and to make matters worse, she'd been on a rollercoaster of emotions concerning him during those years. So no wonder she had her guard up. Duke didn't care how long it took; he'd show her that he was here to stay. Only death would be able to separate him from Duchess this time, and he didn't plan on dying any time soon.

"Are you hungry?" she asked.

He rubbed his stomach and said, "Hell yeah." He wasn't, but just because she'd went through the trouble of cooking for him, he would eat everything she served.

When she sat down across from him at the table, Duke gave her a strange look. "Come on, Duchess. Don't do your boy like that."

"What are you talking about?" she asked.

"Don't treat me like a stranger."

Duchess didn't realize she was doing that. It felt too good to be true to have Duke back in her life, sitting across from her in her home. She was afraid to revel in it... afraid that if she did, something would rip him from her again, and she wouldn't be able to survive losing Duke for a third time. That would absolutely break her beyond recovery.

"This is just crazy, you know? It's like I can't believe you're really here right now. After all this time... everything that's happened... I honestly thought the book was closed on the Duke and Duchess love story," she said honestly.

Duke frowned because he hated that Duchess could ever

feel that way. "That could never happen, Duchess."

"That's easy for you to say because you didn't go through what I was forced to endure. You didn't have to look in the love of your life's eyes and hear them tell you they feel nothing for you and never will."

Duke almost dropped his fork. The chicken rigatoni he chewed suddenly tasted like rubber.

"That wasn't me, Duchess," he felt the need to remind her.

"I know," she said. "I'm just saying, that's why I never thought this could happen." She motioned between them with her hand.

"Duchess, what's meant to be will always be."

"How do you know we're meant to be?"

Duke smiled at her. "Because no matter what obstacle was thrown in our paths, we always found our way back to each other."

Duchess knew Duke was her soulmate; God specifically designed him just for her. Him sitting across from her right now after everything they'd been through proved what she always felt was true.

Her eyes tore over Duke. Everything about him was just as she remembered. Time stood still then reversed back into the past to the day she fell in love with him, to the day he asked her to be his wife.

Now, everything was coming full circle.

She stared into Duke's face, admiring every one of his beautiful features. Then, her eyes traced down to his broad shoulders and his muscular arms then froze as soon as she noticed his cracked and bruised knuckles.

"Duke! What happened?"

Duke followed her eyes and saw that she'd peeped his swollen knuckles. He didn't want to lie to her, but at the same time, he wasn't sure how she'd take the news. She'd known Shai as long as she'd known Duke. He'd been like a brother to Duchess as well.

"I had to kill Shai tonight," Duke said without emotion as if Shai hadn't meant anything to him, as if Shai had been merely a stranger.

Duchess's fork fell from her fingers and made a loud clamping sound as it hit the plate. "Duke! Why?" She shook her head. "What are you even saying right now?"

"He tried to kill me, Duchess. He's the whole reason we in this mess right now. Nigga was supposed to be my brother, and he looked me in my eyes and shot me." Duke pounded his chest with every word.

So Ford had been right all along to suspect Shai. Duchess didn't want to believe it. She'd pushed the thought to the furthest corner of her mind, but now she had to face it. If Duke killed Shai, then it had to be true. She was afraid to ask the question making circles in her thoughts.

"Yeah, Jerrika knew," Duke said before she could even ask it. "Shai said she put him up to it, and I believe him. Bitch always was jealous of you. You just couldn't see it."

Tears welled in Duchess's eyes. She'd long given up on her friendship with Jerrika, but it completely broke her heart to know that Jerrika had wished such pain to Duchess. To know that Jerrika looked her in her face every day following Duke's funeral, knowing that she was the one who put him in that grave.

"Is she dead?" Duchess asked, preparing herself for the answer.

"Not yet."

Duchess wouldn't plead for Jerrika's life. She wouldn't even ask Duke to make it painless or quick. Jerrika deserved everything that was coming to her. She'd been the worst kind of person to have in Duchess's circle, pretending she had Duchess's back and to love her like a blood sister only to plot on her demise as soon as Duchess's defenses were down.

Duchess had never wished death on anyone, not even her worst enemy, but tonight, she wished that very thing for the bitch who wore a mask of friendship.

Duke hated that Duchess was crying over that traitorous bitch, Jerrika. He hated that he even had to bring her up, because the entire atmosphere had shifted. He refused to have their night of reunion ruined. He got up from the table and walked over to Duchess. She wiped her eyes with a napkin, and he grabbed her hand.

"Don't cry, Duch. You know a nigga hate it when you cry. I wish it didn't have to be like this, but Jerrika has to die."

"I'm not crying because Jerrika has to die. I'm crying because I know I'm about to catch my first body."

Duke could have been knocked over by a feather. The Duchess he knew had always been timid and demure, the epitome of a lady. The Duchess sitting before him was a savage, and the shit was so sexy to him.

The heat of undeniable desire began to burn furiously between them at that moment. Duchess sucked in a breath as she stared into Duke's eyes and saw a reflection of the same way she felt. The time they'd lost no longer mattered. The past and present came colliding together at the speed of light. Lust danced violently between them.

Duke blinked, but he didn't look away. He admired everything about this new Duchess. Two years may have passed, but she looked exactly the same as the day he boarded that plane to the DR. No, that wasn't true. She was more beautiful now. Long gone was the air of naivety Duchess once carried. It'd been replaced with the glow of a survivor, the hardness that only someone who'd traveled to hell and back could carry.

Duchess felt vulnerable and naked under the intensity of Duke's gaze. She was vibrantly aware of the way his eyes drank in every part of her. She wondered what he saw when he stared at her. She wished she could read his thoughts like a novel, because he was both familiar and unfamiliar to her.

There was a painful ache of desire building inside of her, the ache of need that only Duke could soothe. It'd been so long since she felt the heaviness of Duke's body on top of her, but she never forgot how it felt. Right now, her body craved his touch.

Duke didn't know Duchess's situation with Brian, and truthfully, he didn't give a fuck. In his eyes, Duchess belonged to him and always would. The thought of her with another man felt like acid being poured on his brain. He had to erase every trace of that nigga from his Duchess. He reached for her and was glad when she didn't pull away or resist his touch.

"Come here, Duch." He pulled her to her feet and wrapped his arms around her. She fit inside his arms like the missing piece to a puzzle. His fingers traced the vertebrae beads of her spine, throwing fuel to the fire already inside of her.

Duchess felt a thousand sensations racing through her body. She shivered at the feeling of Duke's touch against her skin. She breathed him in, and the scent of his masculinity tickled her nose. She leaned deeper into his touch and moaned as his kisses left her earlobe and traced down her neck. "Duke," she moaned. Her voice was throaty and full of desire.

"Do you still love me, Duchess?"

His question made her cry, but she didn't know why. "I never stopped," she answered.

Duke always been a gangster, but it was something about Duchess that turned him putty in the palm of her hand.

"Fuck," he groaned, and he sounded as if he were in physical pain. "I need you, Duchess."

"You have me. All of me."

Duke picked her up with little effort, and she wrapped her legs around his waist. Their lips connected, their tongues engaging in a wrestling match of desire and lust.

The longer they kissed, the more Duchess felt the fragments of her heart being pieced back together.

Duke walked to her bedroom and laid her onto the bed. The dim streetlights peeking through the blinds illuminated the room just enough, so they were able to see one another in the dark. Duchess took a handful of Duke's shirt in her fist and pulled him closer. She spread her legs wide, inviting him entrance into the deepest part of her.

Duke feasted on her lips. He wasn't sure where he'd been when he was trapped as Demarcus, but this was where he belonged.

Clothes were tossed and ripped off at a rapid speed. Lips to lips, chest to chest, fingers and legs intertwined—they couldn't get any closer than they were. Duke was harder than he'd ever been, desperate to be back home inside of Duchess.

"I love you, Duke," she whispered breathlessly. She'd been so afraid to let herself go like this. Too afraid that once she'd given in, her life would be ripped from beneath her feet once again. But as she wrapped her legs around Duke, who refused to pull his lips from hers, she knew this was permanent. As he slid inside her with ease, joining their bodies as one flesh, she knew nothing would ever separate her from this man again.

CHAPTER TWENTY-FOUR

Auri beat her fist against Duchess's door. She'd been knocking for what felt like forever. She wondered if the young chick from the diner had gamed her out of four hundred dollars and given her a bogus address.

Levi had started to cry, so she bounced him on her hip. He was sleepy and cranky, adding to Auri's already aggravated mood.

"Open the door, you fuckin' bitch!" She hollered as she beat on Duchess's door. It was obvious no one was home, but she didn't stop knocking. She wanted to kick the door down because she was so pissed. She was looking to pin blame on someone for the state of her ruined life, and Duchess was the perfect candidate.

The sound of the door being unlocked shocked Auri. She pulled her fist from the door just as Duchess swung it open.

Auri took in Duchess's sudden appearance. She stood there in a leopard print silk robe tied tightly around her tiny waist. She wasn't what Auri expected, but nevertheless, she was a beautiful woman. With dark skin as silky as the robe she wore, Duchess's complexion was flawless. Her hair was tousled as if she'd just been freshly fucked. On top of that, she had that post orgasm glow. Auri sneered at her, a hatred she'd never felt for anyone before began bubbling inside of her.

"Can I help you!" Duchess snapped. She didn't know who this chick was or why she was beating on her door like a damn fool in the middle of the night. She was seconds from cursing this chick out when Duke came up behind her.

"What the fuck you doing here?" Duke asked, his tone tempered and vexed.

Duchess looked from Duke to the woman at her door, and immediately, she knew who this woman was. She looked at the child in her arms and easily saw Duke all over the boy. Something in Duchess's heart began to rip. Not even five minutes earlier, she lay in Duke's arms as they spoke of their plans for the future. Now, Auri was at her door with every intention of destroying all those plans.

Auri wasn't dumb enough to expect a warm welcome from Duke, but she also hadn't expected the glare of death he gave her. "What do you mean what am I doing here? Did you forget that you're a father? You haven't reached out to Levi in two fuckin' weeks!" Auri said.

Duke glared at Auri. He didn't know her, but he hated her. She didn't need to pop up at Duchess's place in order for him to take care of his seed. He had plans of sending for Levi, but first he needed to iron shit out in Dallas. There were things he had to put in place before he brought his son to America.

"I know what I did was fucked up, but don't take it out on Levi, because he didn't ask to be here!" Auri screamed loudly. She sounded and looked like a crazed woman. Her eyes bucked out of her head, and her voice was unnecessarily loud.

Duke grabbed her by the arm and pulled her inside the apartment before the neighbors called the police on her for disturbing the peace.

"You right, what you did was fucked up!" Duchess snapped. She glared at Auri, disgusted that she'd ever had the chance to lay her filthy hands on Duke, disgusted that she had the nerve to come to her house wearing that wedding ring as if she'd had any right to marry Duke. Duchess wanted to knock this woman's head off her shoulders.

"I'm not talkin' to you, bitch!" Auri said. "This is between my husband and me." She lifted her left hand and wiggled her ring finger in Duchess's face. "Why don't you go find a man of your own instead of breaking up a happy home, you home-wrecking slut!"

Duchess would have laughed in Auri's face if anger didn't have such a hold on her. She looked at Duke. "Get your son," she told him. Her voice was flat and in a tone that Duke had never heard from Duchess before. He didn't ask any questions; he just took Levi from Auri's arms.

"Good," Duchess said as soon as Levi was safe in Duke's arms. "'Cause I'm about to fuck this bitch up."

Auri had been in more fist fights than she could count. Plenty of chicks had tried her at the strip club, making the mistake of thinking her pretty looks meant she was weak. Nothing about Duchess intimidated Auri. She'd fought bigger bitches for pettier reasons, so if Duchess wanted to take it there, Auri was glad to give her the ass whupping she desired.

"Bitch, please!" Auri said with the roll of her eyes. Her accent was always at its thickest when she was pissed off. "You don't wanna see me. Trust."

Auri's show of bravado meant nothing to Duchess. She would have been able to handle it if this was just a woman Duke had cheated on her with. She could have gotten over that, but no. This was the woman who deliberately conned Duke at his weakest moment. She'd stolen things that should have only belonged to Duchess. Auri had this ass whupping coming.

Duchess didn't say another word. Time was out for talking. She lunged toward Auri with the ferocity of a tiger. Auri saw the punch way before it connected. She could have dodged it. She *should* have dodged it because as soon as it made impact with her nose, she felt it break. The pain was reminiscent of childbirth, and Auri howled like a wounded animal in the wild. She could taste the metallic taste of blood running from her nose onto her lips. She couldn't dwell on the pain long because Duchess was kicking her ass!

She kicked, punched, and rolled on the ground with Duchess. They bumped into furniture, knocking pictures off tables and walls. Auri grabbed a fistful of Duchess's hair and yanked with all her strength. She felt the hair ripping from Duchess's scalp and hoped it hurt enough to get Duchess off her. Auri had never lost a fight in her life, but Duchess was giving her the business.

Two years of pent-up anger, resentment, and frustration was being released through Duchess's fists. Auri wasn't the cause of what happened to Duke, but she'd contributed in such a way that unnecessarily prolonged his illness.

Her robe had ripped, and she was damn near butt naked fighting Auri, but she didn't care. Duchess spoke with every hit like a mother punishing an unruly child. "Gon'. Come. To. My. House. With. The. Bullshit."

"That's enough, girl. That's enough!" Duke picked Duchess up by her waist and pulled her off Auri, kicking and screaming.

Auri scrambled to a safe distance away from Duchess. "You let this bitch beat on me like that in front of my son!"

"You shoulda never brought your ass to my house, bitch!" Duchess screamed, still kicking as Duke carried her to the bedroom.

Auri was smart enough not to follow. She didn't want a round two with Duchess. When she saw Duchess again, it would come down to gunplay. No one would put their hands on Auri like that and live to talk about it. She scrambled to her feet and retrieved Levi from the couch. Somehow during the commotion, he'd managed to fall asleep. She swooped him into her arms and headed toward the door.

"Where you going?" Duke asked before she could leave.

"Fuck you," she said without looking back at him.

"Leave my son here," he demanded.

Auri laughed, but it was without humor and full of bitterness. "Puh-leez! You'll be lucky if you ever see him again."

She walked out of Duchess's apartment with an ego as bruised and battered as her body.

CHAPTER
TWENTY-FIVE

Everyone in the room looked at KP like he smoked dope. The members of GMB only agreed to meet with him today because he said he had info on who killed Shai. What they didn't expect was for him to come up in the spot talking about Duke being alive. Most of them were ready to rush the little nigga because they took his words as a sign of disrespect to their fallen leader.

"Come on, KP. I stuck my neck out for you by calling this meeting," Cristo said. "Now you making me look crazy as hell."

"I ain't lying! Duke is alive! He's the one who killed Shai," KP said, knowing if he hadn't been there, he probably wouldn't have believed it either. It'd been two long years since anyone in this room had seen Duke. It was no wonder they thought he was full of shit.

"Man, somebody put a bullet in this nigga's mouth!" somebody yelled from across the room.

"That won't be necessary," Duke said as he calmly entered the room, looking every bit of the boss he was.

The room went silent. No one dared to move or say a word. Ford and Gunz walked into the spot as well, but no one even noticed because their eyes were stuck on Duke.

"What? Y'all acting like y'all seen a ghost or something," Duke cracked, breaking the heavy pressure in the room.

THE DUKE AND DUCHESS OF DALLAS 2

The room erupted in laughter and a hundred questions all at once. A few members of GMB got up and hugged Duke. Everyone had questions.

"It's a long story," Duke said.

"Well, you better start at the beginning," Cristo said, still unable to believe he was actually talking to Duke.

The room went silent as Duke told the story of where he'd been the last two years. With the exception of a few curse words being shouted every now and then, no one interrupted him.

"Damn," Cristo said while shaking his head after Duke had finished.

"So, if anybody knows where we can find that bitch Jerrika, let us know," Ford said.

"She disappeared into thin air," Cristo said. He'd been unable to reach Jerrika ever since the day after Shai had been killed, and that was two weeks ago. "I been on the lookout for her because I thought whoever killed Shai was coming for her, but after what you just told us, I see why the bitch ran." Cristo shook his head. He always knew something wasn't right about Jerrika, but he never thought she could be this grimy.

"I need the hood to know what she did to Duke," Ford said. "The bitch put a bounty on my head, so we doubling the price for whoever can bring her to us alive."

"Alive?" somebody asked from the back.

"Yeah. I don't want her killed. That pleasure belongs to someone else," Duke said, remembering what Duchess said that night. The corners of his mouth lifted into a devious smile.

"Wait a minute. Y'all saying y'all putting four hundred grand on the bitch's head?" Cristo asked for clarification.

"Dats right," Ford said.

Cristo shook his head. It was over for Jerrika. He hoped for her sake she was thousands of miles away from Dallas. She deserved every piece of the karma pie Duke was going to serve her, but Cristo didn't want to be anywhere around to witness it because he knew it would mirror a scene out of a horror movie.

"Oh yeah, one more thing," Duke said before the members of GMB could disperse. "Let the hood know the muthafuckin Duke of Dallas is back."

The room erupted in hoots and applause because everyone knew the city was about to be lit like never before.

Brian handed Duchess the key to her place.

This wasn't what he thought he'd be doing when she called and asked him to come over. In fact, it was the complete opposite of what he expected. He'd done what he said he would. He didn't call or text her. He gave her space to clear her head. Two weeks of no contact, and she'd decided to rip his heart out of his chest as if it never meant anything to her at all.

"I'm so sorry, Brian," Duchess said before exchanging the engagement ring for the key to her place.

He stared at her hand, not wanting to take the ring or believe this was happening.

Duchess felt like shit. She didn't want to hurt Brian because he'd been there for her when she needed him the most. He'd loved her when she didn't want to be loved. He'd nurtured every broken piece of her heart and made her believe in love again, and this was how she repaid him.

"So that's it? It's over? Just like that?" Brian asked, his

voice cracking.

"I'm sorry."

"It's Duke, huh?" Brian shook his head. "Who am I kid- ding? It's always been Duke! Even when we thought he was dead, it was Duke! Always in between us, keeping us from progressing forward in this relationship."

Duchess didn't know what to say. She just wanted Brian to give her back her key, take his ring, and go. She didn't want things to get awkward. She didn't want to see the hurt she'd caused, but he was shoving it in her face, making sure she saw it.

"I hope he makes you happy," Brian said, but it was obvi- ous he didn't mean that. He snatched his ring from Duchess and walked toward her door, knowing he'd never walk through it again. He turned to take one last look at Duchess. "I just hope for your sake he doesn't get caught up in some more street shit and get himself killed for real this time."

Duchess was too shocked to even respond. By the time she recovered enough to say something, Brian was gone.

THREE MONTHS LATER...

CHAPTER
TWENTY-SIX

Jerrika no longer resembled herself. Long gone was the flawless, waist-length blonde weave and designer threads. These days, she wore clothes from the Goodwill and garage sales. Sometimes, it shocked her just how drastic her life went to shit, but that's how it was when you were on the run. Everyone in Dallas and even the surrounding cities were looking for Jerrika. Word on the street was Duke had a four hundred-thousand-dollar price tag on her head. That kind of money was unheard of. She was a walking lottery ticket.

The only thing that gave Jerrika a little peace of mind was she now looked nothing like herself. Her clothes were dirty and hung off her smaller frame. She'd lost all her curves from the stress of being on the run. Plus, she was no longer eating five-star meals. Jerrika, the former self-proclaimed First Lady of GMB now had to dumpster dive for food. Some days, she wondered if death would be better than this.

She tapped her foot impatiently as she waited in the seemingly never ending line at the homeless shelter. She silently prayed it wouldn't be full by the time she made it to the door. She couldn't endure another night on the street. It was winter, and the coat she wore was so thin that she might as well have not had it on.

She looked over her shoulder out of habit. Even though she was now in Houston, over two hundred miles from Dallas, she feared being spotted. She didn't have enough money to flee further than Houston, but as soon as she scrounged up enough funds, she was getting the fuck out of Texas!

The wind whipped past, stinging Jerrika's face and bringing tears to her eyes. It was too cold to sleep under a bridge tonight, not to mention, unsafe. She'd nearly been raped the few times she had to sleep outside.

The bitter taste of regret lingered in her mouth as she thought about the days she laughed at Duchess when she thought Duchess was going broke. Not even once had Jerrika offered a helping hand to her friend. Instead, she laughed and basked in Duchess's misfortune, especially when she found out Duchess was working in a bakery. What Jerrika would do now for the opportunity to work in a bakery. Hell, to work anywhere!

The sound of disappointment echoed throughout the line, so Jerrika knew that meant the shelter was full for the night. She cursed, and her dwindling will to live decreased even more.

The crowd of people dispersed, and Jerrika followed a group of women who walked away together. She knew safety came in crowds, so she walked fast to catch up with them. When she realized they were headed toward the street that was known for prostitution, she stopped in her tracks.

Her stomach growled loudly, but she didn't need the reminder that she was starving. She hadn't eaten in two days. She was cold, hungry, dirty, and sleepy. She knew karma was a bitch, but that bitch was being unnecessarily cruel to her.

Sure, she'd wanted Duke dead, but did he actually die? No! Shouldn't that have eased some of the bad karma headed in her direction? Sure, she laughed at Duchess going broke, but Duchess hadn't ever ended up on the streets. The only reason she'd killed Tommy was because he was going to kill her. It was self-defense!

Engulfed in her own pity party, she hadn't noticed she was

now standing on the stroll with several other women, shivering to keep warm in the blistering winter cold. The sound of a car blaring its horn snapped her out of her thoughts.

The man sitting behind the driver's seat of the old Chevy stared right at Jerrika. A chick wearing pleather thigh high boots walked up to his car, only to be quickly dismissed.

"He wants you," she said as she walked past Jerrika and sat down on the cold concrete.

Jerrika wasn't the same woman she'd been just three months ago, but she hadn't fallen far enough to start selling her ass! She curled her face in disgust, but the merciless wind slapped her face, quickly wiping that expression away. The lure of sitting in a warm car was too good to pass up. Maybe she could earn enough dollars to buy a warm meal tonight. She was sure her stomach almost touched her back.

She licked her dry and chapped lips before walking toward the car. The guy behind the wheel wasn't ugly, but he also wasn't the kind of guy Jerrika would have ever gone for. His car was over fifteen years old, he was overweight, and the goofy oversized grin verified that he was a lame.

"How much for some top, momma?" he asked while licking his lips.

Jerrika wasn't sure what was appealing about her to this man. She was dirty and stanking, but this nigga looked at her like she was Beyoncé's sister or something.

"Uhhh…" She didn't know how much to charge. She couldn't believe she was about to give this dude head in exchange for money, but she was relieved that's all he wanted.

"I'll give you twenty-five dollars," he offered.

Jerrika was offended but not offended enough not to get in his car. The warmth from the heat blaring through his vents felt so good, she shuddered. "Money first," she said.

The man gave her a look. "You know better than that."

Actually, she didn't. She'd never done this before in her life.

He pulled away from the busy street and onto one that looked almost deserted. He parked the car in an empty, dark shopping center and leaned his seat back. He unzipped his pants and pulled his short dick out. He gripped it with one hand while reaching for Jerrika's head with the other.

She took several deep breaths to calm her nerves. She was having second thoughts. This wasn't her; she was better than this! How did her life go from pushing Bentleys to sucking dick in an old ass Chevy? She wanted to cry, but she was too dehydrated to even form tears.

She closed her eyes and leaned into the man's lap. He smelled sweaty and musty enough for her to gag.

"Eat this dick, bitch."

Jerrika closed her eyes and did as he said, all the while wishing she was dead.

CHAPTER TWENTY-SEVEN

Duchess sat in the passenger seat of Duke's car, silently fuming. For the past couple of months, Duke met Auri in a Denny's parking lot to pick up Levi. Even though Duchess had whupped her ass something serious, she still couldn't stand Auri, and the feeling was mutual.

Levi, on the other hand, she adored. At first, she worried that she wouldn't care for the boy. She worried that her resentment would keep her from even being able to look at him. That wasn't the case though. Duchess fell head over heels in love with the happy baby. Levi always smiled and giggled whenever Duchess held him. She didn't think she was ready for kids, but Levi made her a mother, and she loved every moment she spent with him.

Duke locked Levi into his car seat before getting into the car. "Something wrong with her, man," he said.

"What she do now?" Duchess asked while rolling her eyes. Her intuition had been right: Auri was the baby momma from hell. When she wasn't threatening to take Levi and run back to the Dominican Republic, she was telling Duke how much she loved and missed him. Other times, she would call in the wee hours of night claiming some kind of emergency, only for Duke to get there and find out the reason for the call was something as petty as Levi refusing to eat a banana.

Sometimes, Duchess could swear she saw Auri or someone who closely resembled her in the parking lot of Duchess's college. She had a nagging suspicion Auri was following her but didn't want to sound paranoid, so she never brought it to Duke's attention.

Besides, Duchess was sure Auri didn't want a round two with her hands.

"She ain't do nothing," Duke said. "It's just the way she acting. She acting weird as hell."

"You don't really know her, Duke. Maybe that's just how she acts."

"Naw," Duke said, shaking his head. "Something is off about her." Duke made it up in his mind right then and there to holla at Rico later tonight about his cousin. He couldn't put his finger on it, but something was definitely not right with Auri.

Auri screamed as loud as her voice would allow. She slapped the steering wheel as she watched Duke and Duchess pull off the parking lot. Every time she was forced to look at that bitch, another piece of her sanity chipped away.

Auri convinced herself that Duchess had somehow caused Duke's memories to return. She had it worked up in her head that Duchess was some kind of witch and had worked black magic on Demarcus and that was the reason he had no memory of her.

Auri began to worry if Levi was even safe with Duke when Duchess was around. She'd been in Texas for three months, but she didn't plan on staying here much longer. She was going back home, and she was taking Duke with her. She just had to figure out how to get rid of Duke and bring Demarcus back.

Jerrika felt dirty.

She took a shower so hot that it almost scalded her skin. She stood in the hot shower so long that the water turned cold. Still, she felt dirty.

She didn't want to think about the things she'd done with Frank tonight. She'd done things she would never repeat for the promise of a warm meal and warm bed.

"Hurry up and come out of there!" Frank hollered from the other side of the door.

Jerrika shut the shower off and reluctantly climbed out. She hoped Frank wasn't trying to go again. She was already raw from the hours of rough sex she had to endure. She shook her head, wishing she would have just got out of the car after giving him the blow job. Now, she was stuck in a hotel room with him, and she was sure the nigga had popped a Viagra or something because he'd been hard since they got here which was almost five hours and three nuts ago.

There wasn't a lot of things Jerrika regretted in her life, but tonight, she was sorry she let greed and envy overtake her life. If she hadn't been so greedy for Shai to take Duke's place and so envious of Duchess's life, she wouldn't have plotted Duke's death, wouldn't have been on the run for her life, and she damn sure wouldn't be held up in a fifty-dollars-a-night hotel room with a nigga offering her food in exchange for sex.

She towel-dried her body and hair before wrapping that same towel around her. She walked out of the bathroom and wanted to burst into tears when she saw Frank lying on the bed still naked with his dick in his hand.

"Please... I need some sleep," she said.

Frank looked at her as if she was crazy. He didn't pay for this room for her to sleep. He eyed her thin body and licked his lips. "Baby, we got all night to sleep."

Jerrika would rather sleep under a bridge than spread her legs for Frank again. She couldn't handle the degradation any longer.

"Where yo' man at, anyway?" Frank asked.

"I don't have one."

"So, if I didn't scoop you up tonight, where would you be right now?"

She shrugged, not wanting to admit she was homeless.

"You on drugs?"

"Hell naw!" Jerrika knew she didn't look like herself, but she didn't look like a dope fiend.

"I'm headed to Arizona in the morning. You wanna ride with me?"

Jerrika's eyes bulged. It wasn't as far from Texas as she wanted to get, but it was far enough. "Yeah! I was trying to get outta Houston anyway."

Frank smiled. He smelled the desperation on Jerrika as soon as she got inside his car. He knew if he waved a few dollars, she would be down for whatever. He thought it would take some convincing to get her to tag along with him, but she'd damn near jumped at his offer.

"Alright. I guess we can call it a night then. We got a long drive ahead of us tomorrow," he said.

Jerrika smiled. Maybe just maybe things were finally turning around for her.

CHAPTER TWENTY-EIGHT

Duke had to get used to this new Duchess. Baby girl was more head strong than she'd ever been. Since taking over GMB like he'd never left, Duke was back on top. He talked Duchess into quitting the bakery, but she refused to drop out of school. She took classes three days a week. Even though he would have preferred she quit school, he admired her ambition. She was determined to have her own even though her man was the Duke of Dallas.

Duke's reputation had always been legendary in Dallas, but now that he was back after everyone thought he was dead, he became almost mythical. Whenever he spoke, shit moved, which was why he couldn't understand what was taking so long for Jerrika to be found.

Duke hated to leave anything unfinished, and this shit with Jerrika irked the hell out of him.

Duchess kissed him before grabbing her backpack. She was headed to her night class at Eastfield College. "Stop pouting," she teased.

"I can't help it. I hate to see you walk away."

Duchess giggled and walked out of her new home toward her new car. Duke didn't understand why she refused to stop going to school, especially since he provided her with everything her heart desired, but this was something she had to do.

Never again would she find herself in a helpless situation. She didn't plan on being only Duke's kept woman this time.

She headed to school, checking her rearview several times because she could have sworn a black Nissan Versa, which just so happened to be the exact color, make, and model of Auri's car, following close behind her.

Duchess didn't believe in coincidences. She'd learned to listen to her gut, and right now, it was screaming at her.

The Nissan sped up so fast it looked like it was about to rear end Duchess's car. The driver slammed on the brakes before the cars could collide.

"What the fuck?" Duchess said, eyes darting from in front of her to her rearview mirror. "This bitch really is crazy!"

The Nissan switched lanes abruptly and sped up until it was side to side with Duchess. Sure enough, when she turned to see who was behind the wheel, it was Auri smiling at her, looking crazed and maniacal. Her hair was all over her head and she had bright red lipstick smeared across her lips.

Before Duchess realized what was happening, Auri veered into her lane. Duchess had to hastily swerve to keep from being side swiped. She cursed as soon as she realized Auri was trying to run her off the road.

Two things ran through Duchess's mind at once: She prayed Levi wasn't in the car, with Auri driving like a complete maniac, and she knew without a doubt that Auri was trying to kill her.

This was the first time in three months that Jerrika felt

at ease. She threw her head back, brought the thin jacket to her chin, and closed her eyes as Frank drove. She didn't know how far Arizona was from Texas but knew it wasn't far enough. Duke's reach was long and far. She would forever be looking over her shoulder.

She was at ease enough to fall asleep as Frank drove. When he wasn't hounding her for sex, he was actually a pretty cool guy. He asked her a lot of questions about her family and what happened in her life to turn her to prostitution. Jerrika had always been a good liar, so she fed him a bunch of bullshit about running away from home from a sexually abusive father at a young age. She wanted to play on Frank's sympathy, hoping he'd feel bad enough not to ask her for anymore sex. As soon as they made it to Arizona, she was ditching his fat ass.

Jerrika wasn't sure how long she'd been asleep, but once she opened her eyes, she saw it was dark outside, and the car was parked. She yawned and stretched her arms. She couldn't remember the last time she slept that good. Having a four-hun-dred-thousand-dollar hit out on you meant a lot of sleepless nights.

She checked out her surroundings and couldn't tell where they were. It was so dark, but it looked like they were parked at some abandoned warehouse. Frank wasn't in the car, but Jerrika knew when he returned, he'd ask for some head or something. It was the only reason he'd park in such a deserted area.

She sucked her teeth. "I'm sicka his ass."

She debated if she should just get out of the car and hitch-hike the rest of the way to Arizona. Her hand was on the door handle when it was suddenly yanked open. She screamed at the shock, screamed because she was being yanked out of the car, and the man snatching her out of the car was... Tommy!

"Long time no see, bitch!" he growled.

"Wait, wait, wait!" Jerrika screamed as she tried to keep

herself from being dragged from the car, but it was useless. Tommy was a lot stronger than her. "I thought you were dead! I killed you! How are you here? I killed you!"

Gunz didn't know what the hell Jerrika was talking about. "You killed me?"

As soon as he said it, it hit him. Worse than any sucker punch. It felt like a gunshot to the chest. He looked down at Jerrika, who screamed, kicked, and cried, trying to yank out of his grasp.

"It was you?" He tried to make sense of what she'd just said. "You killed my brother?"

Jerrika realized her mistake too late. This wasn't Tommy. This was his crazy, psychotic twin brother, Gunz. She had just admitted to killing Tommy.

She opened her mouth to offer a rebuttal but was silenced when Gunz punched her right in the face, immediately putting her to sleep.

"This bitch is trying to kill me!" Duchess yelled into her cell.

"What? Who?" Duke asked.

"Auri!"

"Auri?"

"Yes! She's trying to run me off the road!"

"What the fuck!" Duke couldn't believe this. Never mind the timing was all off. He'd just gotten the call from Gunz that Frank, the man in Houston who'd spotted Jerrika, had safely delivered her to one of their warehouses. He was on his way there when Duchess called him with this bullshit.

"Baby, she's driving crazy as hell. She's already rammed me from behind twice!"

"Duchess, listen to me. Take the next exit."

"Exit? What if she follows me? What if she has a gun? What if she's waiting for me to come to a stop so she can shoot me?" Duchess was frantic.

"Calm down, baby girl, and listen to me. I put a piece under your seat. It's loaded. Take the safety off like I showed you. Take the next exit, and if she follows you, do what you gotta do."

Could Duchess kill Auri? *Hell yeah*, she quickly decided. The chick had snapped! She'd gone crazy!

"I'm gonna stay on the phone with you. Tell me what exit you're taking. I'm on my way."

Duchess took the first exit she came to and told Duke. She checked in her rearview for Auri but was surprised when she didn't see the black Nissan behind her.

"Wait… she's gone."

"She's gone?" Duke had hopped into his truck. He'd made it up in his mind that tonight was going to be a bloody one. It no longer mattered that Auri was the mother of his son or that she was connected to Rico. She crossed the line when she came for Duchess.

"You sure?" he asked.

"Yeah, I'm sure. I don't see her anymore. I'm pulled over at a RaceTrac. She's gone." Duchess had the gun in her hand while she looked out the window for Auri. There was no trace of her. She released several deep breaths, trying to ease her nerves that were now fried to a crisp.

Duke would handle Auri, but that had to wait. "Babe, I

need you to skip class tonight."

Under any other circumstance, Duchess would have put up a fight or some kind of argument, but not tonight. Her mind was all over the place, and there was no way she'd be able to concentrate in class. "OK."

"I need you to meet me somewhere," Duke said. "That package you ordered arrived."

Duchess immediately recognized Duke speaking in code. She didn't know what he was referring to, but she knew not to ask too many questions. She entered the address he gave her into her GPS and headed there.

CHAPTER TWENTY NINE

Jerrika's eyes fluttered open. Her head hurt so bad, she immediately shut them. She felt like she'd been hit upside the head with a sledgehammer. She groaned and attempted to touch her head, but she didn't have control of her hands.

Her eyes shot open. She was tied to a chair! She wanted to scream, but she was gagged. Fear gripped her entirely as she remembered what happened. Gunz had somehow found her, dragged her out of the car, and knocked her out! Now he had her bound and gagged in a piss smelling warehouse.

She was as good as dead now. Gunz was Ford's right-hand man. There was no way Gunz had her held here without Ford knowledge. She cried because she was terrified of dying.

She heard the sound of voices and stopped sniveling so she could make out what they were saying. She immediately recognized Frank's voice. He sounded like a man who'd just hit the winning lottery numbers. He was whooping and hollering.

"I ain't never seen this much money in my life! Man, I appreciate this shit, man! Y'all have no idea!"

"Say less," Duke said, and chills sprinted down Jerrika's spine. "We been looking for her for months. You found her and delivered her to us. The money is yours."

Jerrika was about to vomit but knew she couldn't, or she'd choke with the gag in her mouth. She'd been too delirious with hunger and cold to notice Frank's ulterior motives. She'd willingly got in the car with him only to be hand delivered to Duke!

This was it; she was about to die.

"What's up? Why am I here?" Duchess asked as soon as Duke met her outside the warehouse. She ran her hands up and down her arms in attempt to catch some warmth.

Duke took off his jacket and draped it over her. "We found Jerrika."

Duchess hadn't given up hope that they'd find Jerrika, but she couldn't believe it. She looked into Duke's eyes.

"You ready?" he asked, wondering if Duchess had it in her to kill her best friend.

She nodded and followed him inside the warehouse. She wasn't surprised when she saw Ford and Gunz there, but she was shocked when she saw just how bloody Jerrika was.

"Sorry," Duke said. "Gunz found out she killed Tommy. He wanted to body this bitch himself, but I told him you was handling that."

"So I had a lil' fun with her first," Gunz said. He had a psychotic gleam in his eyes that gave Duchess pause. "Big homie wouldn't let me kill her, but I had to get my own revenge... for my brother."

The closer Duchess got to Jerrika, the more she was able to see just what Gunz called fun. There were so many cuts and slices on Jerrika, it was a miracle she hadn't bled out. Gunz was still holding the scalpel in his hand, smiling like a lunatic.

"Leave us," Duchess said.

Ford looked at Duke, and when he nodded, he and Gunz followed Duke out of the room.

Jerrika whimpered and pleaded for death. She'd never known pain like this before. She couldn't survive a second longer this way. She'd already passed out six times, only for Gunz to wake her back up and continue torturing her.

"Duchess... please... help me."

"Shut up!" Duchess snapped. She was disgusted. "Why, Jerrika? I loved you like a sister! Why did you do this to me?"

Jerrika could barely keep her eyes open, let alone give Duchess an answer. She could feel the life being drained from her.

"Why, bitch!" Duchess screamed as she slapped Jerrika across the face. The slap was so hard, Duchess's hand felt like she'd just touched a hot iron.

Jerrika's eyes widened. The slap made her alert and brought her back from the brink of the death she prayed for.

"Why, Jerrika?"

"I don't know!" she shouted. "It wasn't always like this. At first, I loved you... you and Billie. Y'all were my girls. Then you met Duke, and it was like y'all had everything while me and Shai struggled to catch up."

Duchess shook her head.

"I tried to be happy for you. I swear I did, but every day it got harder and harder. I couldn't stop asking myself why you and not me? Why did you get the nigga with the money? Why did you get the nigga that didn't even look at another bitch? Meanwhile, Duke was paying Shai crumbs, and Shai was sticking his dick in any and everything that had a pulse."

"But you were my friend," Duchess said. "How could you

harbor that kinda hate for me?"

Jerrika shrugged. "I just did. I hated you and Duke. I knew if we got rid of Duke, everything would be OK. Shai would be the King of Dallas, and I'd finally get all the things Duke got for you."

Duchess had heard enough. She was repulsed. All this time, she would have never imagined Jerrika held these kind of feelings for her. Being jealous was one thing, but Jerrika had tried to take the one thing that meant the world to Duchess: Duke. There was no way she could forgive that.

She clutched the gun Duke had given her. She took the safety off just like he'd taught her and aimed it at Jerrika.

Jerrika whimpered. "Duchess... I'm sorry..."

Duchess pulled the trigger.

CHAPTER THIRTY

It wasn't the wedding of her dreams. It wasn't the ceremony she'd spent months planning, but nevertheless, it was perfect.

Duke and Duchess left the courthouse as Mr. and Mrs. Kingston. Billie, Gunz, and Ford were their witnesses. Duchess couldn't remember being happier. She didn't need the extravagant wedding gown, the expensive floral arrangements, or the five-star catering. All she needed was Duke, and she had him for the rest of her life.

They hopped in Duke's truck and went to a local diner to eat. Duchess would have never imagined such simple things could make her this happy.

"I still can't believe you gave up the chance to tour with Leela Lennox fine ass for this nigga," Gunz joked.

Duchess shrugged. "It wasn't meant to be."

"I wouldn't say all that," Duke said, pulling his cell phone out. He dialed a number and placed his cell in the center of the table.

"Are you making a video call?" Billie asked.

"Who are you calling?" Duchess asked.

"You'll see," Duke said.

Less than a second later, a beautiful woman with caramel-colored curls appeared on the screen. Duchess shrieked, covering her mouth with her hands.

"I hear congratulations are in order," the woman said, her voice as rich as chocolate.

"Oh my God," Duchess said. "Thank you, Leela Lennox." She looked at Duke, unable to believe he somehow had the contact information for *the* Leela Lennox. He shrugged casually as if he hadn't just video called the biggest pop star in the world.

"Duke told me you guy's story and why you had to abruptly bow out of the tour. You guy's story should be a novel or a movie! I mean, it's the epitome of an epic love story that overcame everything!" Leela said. "I know you're a newlywed and everything, but Duchess, I would love it if you'd join me on the last leg on my tour."

Duchess couldn't scream yes fast or loud enough.

"Awesome!" Leela said with a laugh. "I promise, I won't keep you from you hubby too long."

"What you talkin' about, Leela? I'm going on tour too. You think I'm finna have my wife out there getting groupie love?" Duke cracked.

Everyone at the table laughed, but Duchess knew Duke was dead serious. He fully planned on joining her on tour. Truthfully, she wouldn't have wanted it any other way.

"OK, sounds like a plan. I'll have my tour manager reach out and make the arrangements," Leela said before waving goodbye and ending the video call.

Duchess gawked at Duke. "Oh my God! How did you do that?" She looked at everyone at the table and could tell they all knew what Duke planned. She playfully narrowed her eyes at Gunz. "Is that why you brought up Leela Lennox?"

Gunz laughed and chucked a few pieces of popcorn chicken into his mouth.

Duchess shook her head and returned her eyes to Duke. "Seriously, babe. How'd you pull that off?"

Duke gave her a look. "What you mean? Girl, did you forget you married to the Duke of Dallas?"

Duke carried Duchess over the threshold of their home. He couldn't wait to make love to her as his wife. He fully planned on putting a baby in her tonight. They'd lost two years and had a lot of lost time to make up for.

Duchess giggled and playfully slapped him on his shoulder. "Put me down."

Duke did as she requested and followed her into the kitchen as she fumbled around the wall, looking for the light switch to illuminate the darkness of the room.

"Looking for this?"

Duke and Duchess both froze as the light flipped on and they saw Auri standing in the center of the kitchen, holding an assault weapon.

Duchess's blood ran cold. They hadn't seen or heard from Auri since the night she tried to run Duchess off the road. That also meant Duke hadn't seen his son. He was going crazy out his mind worried about Levi. Auri had gone off the deep end, so he hoped she hadn't harmed their child.

"Where's Levi?" Duke immediately asked.

Auri's head flew in the direction of the master bedroom in the back of the house. "He's fine. He's sleeping."

The feeling of sheer relief flooded through Duchess, almost causing her knees to buckle.

"I packed you a bag," Auri said to Duke. "We have a flight leaving tonight at midnight to the Dominican Republic."

Duke eyed the shakiness of Auri's hand on the dangerous gun. He tried to estimate how long it would take him to get across the room and unarm her. Could he make it in time? Would she shoot Duchess before he could get to her?

"I'm not going anywhere with you, Auri."

Auri flinched as if Duke had slapped her. "You have to! Listen, Demarcus, she's a witch. She put some kinda spell on you to erase the memories you made with me. I have to shoot you right now to make you lose your memories again."

Duke and Duchess exchanged looks.

"That's the only way you can wake up as Demarcus again," Auri said. She looked at Duchess and snarled. "I'm gonna kill this witch, so she'll never be able to cast another spell on you, Demarcus. Don't worry about it."

Oh, she was crazy, crazy! Duchess wished she'd seen it sooner. Her eyes darted to Duke at the sound of a loud bang from the rear of the house.

"What was that!" Auri jumped. She looked around nervously but didn't pull the gun away from its back and forth aim at Duke and then Duchess. "Doesn't matter. Let's just get this over with. Eeny, meeny, miney, moe. Which one should I kill first?" She let the gun land on Duchess. "Maybe the ho."

Duchess inhaled a deep breath and closed her eyes. She couldn't believe this was going down like this. She saw movement from her peripheral. Duke reached for the gun he had behind his suit jacket. Duchess said a silent prayer that he'd be quick enough.

"Or maybe I should shoot you first, Demarcus. That way you can get your real memories back in time for our flight," she said. "Yeah, that's what I'll do. I'll count to three, OK? One...two...thr—"

Bang!

Duchess's eyes shot open. She didn't feel the impact of a bullet, so she hadn't been hit. Her head jolted to Duke. He hadn't been shot either, and he wore an expression of confusion. She turned to see Auri lying on the kitchen floor with a hole in the center of her head.

Duchess screamed. Duke pulled his gun and looked around for the shooter.

Two more shots rang out. Duke grabbed Duchess and threw her to the floor while covering her body with his own, protecting her.

"I loved you, Duchesssssssssss!"

Brian?

Duchess screamed.

Brian appeared out of nowhere, literally holding the smoking gun, but he didn't look like the Brian she knew. He had a crazed expression on his face that looked identical to the one Auri wore before he killed her.

Duke glared at Brian. How did this nigga get in his house? The same nagging feeling of familiarity that he felt the first time he saw Brian that day at Duchess's house, began to poke at Duke as he glowered at Brian.

"Get the fuck up!" Brian demanded.

"Alright, man, chill out," Duke said, calm and collected.

"Don't tell me to chill out!" Brian yelled. "You don't tell me shit! You're supposed to be dead! How the hell are you here right now? I thought we threw you in the fuckin' ocean!"

Time came to a screeching halt. Realization echoed through Duke's ears. That's where he knew this nigga from! Brian was the captain of the boat the day Shai tried to kill him. Brian was the captain who'd helped Shai toss Duke's body overboard. Duke wanted to slap himself for not recognizing this nigga sooner!

"Wait, what?" Duchess said. She ogled Brian.

"Oh yeah, you didn't know about that, huh?" Brian said with a hearty laugh. "Shai reached out to me, offered me a lot of money to come to the DR and help him get rid of a pesky little problem. At first, I turned him down. I even thought about going to the cops... but then I saw you." He smiled at Duchess.

"I saw you, Duchess, and immediately fell in love with you, but you belonged to this piece of shit." He pointed the gun at Duke and then looked back at Duchess. "Seeing you, Duchess, was all the convincing I needed to take Shai up on his offer. When we got back to Dallas, I started following you. I gave you time to grieve, promising myself I wouldn't approach you until you'd gotten over Duke's death. That night in the club when that nigga came after you, I had to step in! It was like fate telling me it was time."

The smile on Brian's face melted as he continued to speak. "It was perfect. Everything was. You were falling in love with me and everything until he came back in the picture. I couldn't believe he was still alive! I mean, I saw Shai shoot him! I helped throw his body overboard for fuck's sake! How was he still alive? I knew I was going to lose you, Duchess. That's why I came to the DR after you."

Duchess shook her head in disbelief. How in the world hadn't she seen just how crazy Brian was before he had a gun pointed at her?

"After I found out about his memory loss, I figured there was still a chance for us, Duchess. I'd planned on running back to Dallas and telling Shai he'd fucked up, but when I saw you in that airport that day looking as if Duke had broken your heart once again, I didn't see the need to tell Shai anything. You were coming home with me."

Brian slapped himself against the head and screamed.

"We were going to get married! But here Duke comes fucking everything up once again!" He narrowed his eyes at Duke, aimed the gun, and pulled the trigger. "But not anymore."

"Noooooooooo!" Duchess screamed as soon as the gun went off. She screamed from the very depth of her soul as Duke hit the ground. She ran to him.

Brian jumped in front of Duchess before she could make it to Duke. He grabbed her and tried to subdue her as she punched and screamed at him.

"Let go of me! Let me go! I hate you! I fuckin' hate you!"

"No you don't, Duchess! You loved me once, so you can love me again. You just need to forget about Duke for once and for all," Brian said. He tried to kiss her, but she fought against him so hard, he was unable to do so. Duchess put up resistance and moved so much that it caused Brian to drop the gun. It went skidding across the floor.

Duchess's eyes followed the gun and so did Brian's. They lunged toward it at the same time. Duchess's reach fell short, and Brian's hands wrapped around the gun. He picked it up from the floor and pointed it at Duchess. "Get up! I don't wanna hurt you, Duchess. I didn't come here for that. I came here to save you... to end that Duke and Duchess of Dallas bullshit for good. You're so much better than that hood love, ghetto fabulous nonsense."

"Bitch, ain't no end to Duke and Duchess, ya pussy ass nigga! This bond is bulletproof," Duke growled from behind Brian.

Brian didn't have time to react. He didn't have time to really process what Duke had just said because seconds later, his brains were all over the living room floor.

EPILOGUE

Duchess raced backstage where Duke waited for her. Sure enough, he was there, standing with a huge bouquet of roses. She ran and jumped into his arms, wrapping her legs around his waist.

"You did it, baby girl," Duke said, chuckling.

"Oh my God! I was so nervous, Duke! I thought I was gonna pass the hell out! Did you see all those people out there?"

"You did good though, Duch. I mean, you sang yo' ass off!"

Duchess blushed. "I can't believe Leela Lennox gave me a solo! Like who does that? Who gives their background singer a chance to sing solo to their sold-out crowd?"

"They gave you a standing ovation," Duke said. "They loved you."

Duchess felt overwhelmed. She hadn't expected this. She'd been on tour with Leela Lennox for six weeks. Tonight's show was the last, and it was in Dallas. Leela surprised Duchess by announcing to the crowd that she wanted to introduce them to the next big superstar.

"Some of you may already know her as the Duchess of Dallas," Leela had said.

Duchess felt her heart in her throat. She didn't think she'd even be able to sing, but she'd done it. She'd pulled it off, and Duke was right; the crowd loved her.

"This is only the beginning," Duke said. "Shit 'bout to take off, Duchess. It can only go up from here."

She smiled and kissed him. She didn't care if she never sang in front of a crowd again. She had everything she would ever need right in her arms.

Life wasn't a fairy tale, but Duchess was living her happily ever after. It'd taken some time to get to the peace she now had. She thought about Jerrika every single day. She did what she had to do, but Duchess had been forever changed the moment she pulled that trigger.

She and Duke were raising Levi and eventually one day, they would have to tell him about his mother. It wouldn't be an easy conversation. The one Duke had with Rico about Auri's death hadn't been either. Even though Duke hadn't been directly responsible for Auri getting killed, there was always the chance Rico would want him to pay for it.

Rico didn't want to go to war with Duke, however. His cousin had caused Duke enough grief, and it was her own fault she had to pay with her life for doing so.

"Nah, for real," Duke said. "I know you put your dreams on hold because of us. And then when you found out I was still alive and stuck in the DR, you put your dreams on hold again for us. You ain't gotta do that, Duch. Go chase your dreams. I'm gonna be right here beside you the whole time. Shit, I'm your biggest fan." Duchess was emotional. "I'm proud of you, Duch. But I ain't the only one."

Duchess was confused by what he meant, but once he stepped aside, she saw two people headed toward them. She gasped when they came closer, and she realized it was her parents. Bennet had Levi in his arms and a huge grin on his face. Pamela even smiled.

"Momma? Daddy?" Duchess couldn't believe it. She looked at Duke, and he grinned back at her.

"You were amazing tonight," Bennet said.

"I always knew you could sing, but you blew me away tonight, Duchess," Pamela said earnestly.

Duke wrapped his arms around Duchess and kissed her forehead. She looked up into his eyes as a thousand questions silently passed between them. How in the world had he managed to talk her parents into coming here?

After everything that Duchess had been through this year, she didn't think anything else could surprise her.

Pamela watched their interaction closely. She knew they loved each other, but witnessing it firsthand was something entirely different. She'd been so wrong about Brian. He'd turned out to be a psychotic piece of work! Could that mean that she had also been so wrong about Duke?

As she stared at the way he looked at her daughter, she got her answer.

It wasn't coincidental Duke just so happened to meet a girl named Duchess. They were meant to be. After everything they'd been through, their love withstood and made it through. Pamela couldn't refute the undeniable.

She swallowed her reservations and decided to finally accept Duke as her son-in-law. She reached for Duchess and hugged her tight.

"I'm so happy for you, Duchess," she said, getting her choked up. "You were right all along. Duke is the one."

Duchess smiled at her mother before returning her attention to her husband. Yes, he was the one. He was her Duke, and she was his Duchess.

The End!

Made in United States
North Haven, CT
29 July 2022

21928225R00124